Welcome to Lakeville . . .

As they walked back toward the house, Aunt Lovenia suddenly clutched Sue's arm, startling her. "What was that?" she whispered.

For a moment, they stood listening. Sue heard nothing but the hum of cars on the lake road. Gently she propelled her aunt on.

"You won't mind sleeping upstairs alone?" Lovenia asked.

Sue laughed. "In this peaceful town?"

"Peaceful!" barked her aunt. "There is more hate per square inch in this town than any place else in the universe . . ."

PUT PLEASURE IN YOUR READING
Larger type makes the difference.
This EASY EYE Edition is set in large, clear type—at least 30 percent larger than usual. It is printed on scientifically tinted non-glare paper for better contrast and less eyestrain.

The Love Campaign

Jeanne Bowman

VALENTINE BOOKS
NEW YORK

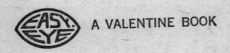 A VALENTINE BOOK

THE LOVE CAMPAIGN

Valentine Books are published by
PRESTIGE BOOKS, INC., 18 EAST 41ST STREET
NEW YORK, N.Y. 10017

Chapter One

She thought of it all the time she was driving to Lakeville. At first her thoughts held no sequence. Her car was overflowing with loggers hitching a ride. Their camps were closed down because of the fire hazard, just as her office, which serviced the camps with labor, had suspended operations.

"Going to have yourself a real vacation, Miss Sue?" asked one.

That really posed the question. Here, when she might have been heading toward cool beaches and the possibility of a summer romance, she was en route to a hot valley and trouble.

Trouble. Now what made her think trouble lay ahead? Her Aunt Lovenia's letters were crammed with tales of wonderful parties, barbecues and picnics, dinners and luncheons. They were also crammed with Milly. With "Milly says . . . "

Who ever heard of anyone having such a wonderful time and still finding hour after hour to write about it?

At the junction where she would turn east and the loggers entrain south, Sue accepted an invitation to lunch with the boys. She sat on a high stool, slippers swinging in space, and consumed a vast hamburger and drank two cups of coffee as thick as the mugs in which it was served.

And she heard a strange voice say, "Wow-zo-wie, what a blond number! Where'd you find her in them-thar hills?"

And she heard a familiar voice say, "Shuddup! That's Miss Thompson."

The strange voice, awed now, whispered, "Good gosh, y'mean that little bit o' girl can handle you lugs?"

"An atom ain't very big either."

She found her car had been serviced when she went out. She waved at the boys, assured she'd see them after the first good rain. And then she sent the car speeding east.

Sometimes she resented being small and a natural blonde—tan colored, she called it. And then her common sense would tell her she was lucky. These men would fight a big, militant woman. Discovering brains in such a feminine package as herself always left the men tongue-tied until she was able to shift them into the timber where they were best fitted to the jobs to which she had assigned them.

Sue reached Lakeville at noon the next day. She came out on the high ridge surrounding the valley, braked, turned off her motor and looked down.

The valley sizzled under the sun's rays. The hills on every side were seared and barren, except for an occasional clump of trees in some canyon.

But at the bottom of the valley, curved like a billowing grey-blue ribbon, lay the lake, rimmed with a black growth of trees and widening at its base to hold the town of Lakeville.

She had visited there once, briefly, two years ago, at the time of the death of her Aunt Lovenia's husband, Ned. It had been winter, as cold then as it would be hot now, and she'd hardly left the house, except for the final services.

"Well, here goes," she said with a sigh which astonished her, and sent the car hurtling down into the valley.

An hour later she was turning off from the hot mountain highway into the cool, tree-shaded streets of Lakeville.

Why, this is lovely, she thought.

Women in light summer dresses, young people in bright sports clothes, cars whisking through filled with people in bathing suits. And at the end of one street she saw a sailboat, sails a big limp, against the blue of the lake waters.

And then she turned onto the lake road and drew up before an old two-storied house.

The house was closed, locked. Sue made her way out to the acre of garden, wandered to the far edge and was rewarded by a neighbor calling, "Looking for Lovey? Probably out to Milly Mack's; practically lives out there nowadays."

"I'm her niece Susan Thompson," Sue returned. "Does she live there nights as well?"

"Well, no," the neighbor conceded. "She usually comes in 'long about the time the young fellow drives in for the late mail. Want to come over here to wait?"

Susan shook her head. "Thanks, I'll wait here."

She'd seen an old wicker couch on the wide front veranda. It was screened from the lake road by vines, but she found, lying on it, that it still gave a cool view of the water. Not that she noticed the view for long. The previous night's tourist cabin had been hot, the bed hard and lumpy.

Maybe this isn't going to be too bad, she thought. Such a lovely, peaceful town. Perhaps the only really peaceful spot in the world right now.

She awakened to voices.

"Lovey," the voice was crisp, "I could almost be annoyed with you. You know what you should do. Why you insist upon staying on, existing, when you might be living fully—"

She didn't hear her aunt's answer, only a young male voice: "Come on, Milly; Lovey's tired."

And then Sue sat up and saw her Aunt Lovenia and felt her heart come up into her throat. What on earth had happened to Lovenia Cantrell? She'd aged beyond belief, and she looked as though the proud spirit which had kept her head at a galliard tilt had been withdrawn.

She saw the car as it roared away. Its motor sang of power, its shining shell of money without end.

Lovenia Cantrell watched it, and Sue watched her, and when the older woman turned toward the

8

house, shoulders drooping, Sue said softly, "Aunt Lovey, it's Sue. I'm here on the porch." And then she spoke louder.

Lovenia Cantrell ran forward then, and when Sue met her, arms were intertwined. "Why, Aunt Lovey, you're crying."

"Relief," murmured Mrs. Cantrell. "I mean that you reached here."

And silently Sue said, But you didn't know I was coming.

And then as though she had been prompted she said, "Sue, why didn't you speak sooner? You could have met my friends. Milly's been so wonderful. And her brother Melvin is such a fine young man. All of the girls in Lakeville are foolish about him."

"And he—" teased Sue.

"Well, as Milly says, she's not going to have him make the mistakes she made."

"Meaning Milly must pass on his girls?"

For the first time Lovenia Cantrell laughed. "Oh, I don't think so. He's quite headstrong."

They went into the house, and Sue thought it more charming than she'd remembered.

"Milly thinks I should sell," Lovenia Cantrell said suddenly.

They had come to the room Sue was to occupy. Sue looked in on daffodil yellow walls, apricot and French blue chintz; a love of a room, she thought it, after her narrow bunk in a room and a half apartment.

"Why?" she asked.

"Well, the place *is* large for one person. And Milly does have a lovely guest room and she'd charge me hardly any rent and I'd be near someone who cared whether I lived or died."

She set her bags down. "And why don't you?"

Lovey Cantrell shook her head. "I can't understand myself. I nearly freeze here winters because I can't afford to heat the big house, yet—oh, I guess it's because Ned and I lived here for our important years. We decorated each room with our own hands, that sort of thing. But we'll speak of that later. I must run down and see what I have in for our dinner."

"You must not," Sue corrected her. "I feel flush. Isn't there some place we can go where we can sit by the lake and be served?"

There was a drive-in on the east side of the lake. But first there was a telephone call.

Sue, coming from a chill shower, stood wrapped in a terry robe and deliberately listened to the one-sided conversation.

"But, Milly, I am not dining on husks tonight. Sue's here. Oh, I've told you about my sister's daughter. Yes, we're all that's left of the family. No, she—well, she's just—she's vacationing."

A moment later she called Sue, and Sue, hurrying down the long stairs, saw her aunt's face was flushed. "It's Milly," she mouthed; "she wants us to come out to the ranch for dinner. Here, she wants to talk to you."

Milly Mack's voice was liquid charm. Had Sue not been so tired she would have responded. But she was tired. She wanted nothing new, especially no new personalities thrust on her.

"I'm sorry, Mrs. Mack," she said with finality; "another time."

When she turned from the telephone she saw her aunt watching her and thought of a small dog she'd once had who had watched the expression on her face to learn if they would or wouldn't go on some delightful adventure.

"Is she annoyed?" Mrs. Cantrell asked.

"I wouldn't know," Sue answered, "nor care. Surely she knows how a person feels who's just driven four hundred miles in intense heat. If she doesn't know or isn't interested—but I'm sorry. She's your friend."

"It's all right. I'll freshen up a bit. It's so nice you can drive, Susan. Ned never trusted me with a car. I would keep watching the scenery instead of the highway."

"You sold the car?"

"Well, sort of."

Sue enjoyed the dinner at the drive-in. She enjoyed it more when she saw her aunt's face. "Ned and I used to do this," Lovenia confided happily. "We didn't have to dress after a day's gardening; just freshen up, then come here and everything was done for us. I do like the fried chicken, don't you?"

"Ummm, good," agreed Sue.

11

"Milly says it's extravagant. Milly says a person could live for a week on what she spends here for one meal."

"Unquestionably," agreed Sue, eyes upon a star intent upon seeing itself in the lake below, "but I'd sooner have one evening of fun and six of spreading the memories on dry bread."

There had been a sudden silence as she spoke, and her voice had rung out clearly. Now from the car next to hers came a strong voice. "There speaks a girl after my own heart."

Sue was startled. She couldn't see into the car, and a moment later it backed out of the circle and pulled away.

Lovenia Cantrell spoke then. "Wasn't that funny?" she asked. "But oh, Susan, so would I."

They drove home along the edge of Lakeville and Sue, looking up the streets, saw them as strips of purple shadows patterned with clusters of yellow lights. Such a peaceful place, she thought.

The old stable had been converted to a garage. Leaving the car there and walking through the kitchen garden to the back door, Sue was startled by the sudden clutch of her aunt's arm.

"What was that?" whispered Lovenia.

For a moment they stood listening. Sue could hear nothing but the hum of cars on the lake shore. Gently she propelled her aunt on. Tomorrow she would suggest a doctor; no one should be this nervous.

"You won't mind sleeping upstairs, alone?"

Mrs. Cantrell asked, after double locking the rear doors, then returning to try them.

"In this peaceful town?" Sue laughed.

"Peaceful?" barked her aunt. "There is more hate per square inch in this town than any place else in the universe."

Sue overslept, wakened to a hot sun pouring in the window, dressed quickly and happily and went racing down the steps, her yellow dress a dancing sunbeam.

They had breakfast in a little summerhouse and Lovenia explained she was due at a church committee meeting. "It's a must or I wouldn't leave you alone. They need my vote. The women are split about evenly, and if I should fail to appear the other side might win."

"Is the issue that serious?"

Lovenia nodded. "It's whether to have a cake or a pie festival." And at Sue's hoot she looked up, some of her old laughter returning. "I know how that must sound. Actually it isn't a matter of cake or pie, but rather, which side has the greater power."

A car horn blared and Lovenia Cantrell scuttled away, leaving Sue to watch and to remember an aunt who had walked, head high, step firm.

There was little Sue could do about the house; her aunt would remain on at the meeting for lunch. She sat a moment at the east window of her room and looked down at the lake. There seemed to be a public beach not too far away.

She'd go for a swim; that would use up part of the time.

She was in a yellow scrap of a bathing suit and half-way down stairs when the telephone rang. It was her aunt. "Sue dear, we're going to Milly Mack's for dinner tonight. . . . Just a minute." She must have turned to talk to someone. "Melvin will pick us up at six-thirty." And abruptly she replaced the receiver.

"Hmm, just like that!" muttered Sue, then tossed her cape about her shoulders and ran out to the car.

There were not many on the beach at this hour of the morning; a few children, a group of small boys intent upon some destructive enterprise, and an occasional couple processing a sun tan.

As far as Sue could see there was no one in the lake; the lifeguard was busy with a group of small fry in a pool. And then she saw the rhythmic rise and fall of arms, and beyond this a dark oblong.

"Good," she said, "a life raft for a destination."

She made a running flat dive and started for the raft, and the guard turned, saw the perfection of her stroke and turned back.

For a little while Sue continued her stroke, and then she faltered, turned over on her back and floated awhile, amazed to find herself so out of condition. When she turned back she looked toward the shore, but it seemed to have receded; the raft was still far away but closer than the shore.

By alternately swimming and floating she

neared the raft. Treading water once, she saw a dark figure silhouetted on it, and was relieved. She'd enjoy company back.

But when she reached the float and went to swing herself up, she found the strength gone from her arms, her legs slung from her hips like leaden weights.

"Give me your right hand, and when I've got a grip, the other." She heard the voice that had sounded from the next car the previous night and looked up to see a mahogany brown figure looming over her; looked into eyes as blue as the summer sky above him.

"Won't I, gladly," she agreed.

He smiled at her when he had lifted her to the float, and when her knees seemed to buckle, eased her down to a sitting position.

"It's farther than it looks," he commented. "I was watching you. I knew you'd be all right if you didn't panic."

"Panic?" She looked up indignantly. "Why should I?"

"You're Lovenia Cantrell's niece, aren't you?" he asked.

Chapter Two

For a moment Sue was furiously angry. Lake-ville must be a hateful place if a complete stranger could speak as this man had.

And then she looked at him and was puzzled. He hadn't meant that as it had sounded. His eyes seemed trying to tell her something.

"My aunt—" she hesitated—"I've never known her to panic."

"Maybe when life knocks the props out from under us—" He left the sentence hanging, and then he smiled. "I think you're man enough to want to ride rather than swim back in. Suppose I go after my canoe and return for you."

"I'm man enough to admit that swim was too much for me."

"First time in this season it would be. How do I know?" He laughed at her questioning eyes. "You're still wearing your winter skin. I'll bring some sun tan oil with me."

He made a clean dive from the float and swam off with a lazy crawl, and Sue, after watching for a moment, lay down in the sun and shuddered in its warmth. . . .

"Okay, Pinkie."

Sue wakened with a start. Pinkie! She sat up indignantly to find a canoe alongside, the man of the blue eyes extending a bottle of oil to her.

"Oh," she said as she glanced down at herself, "another hour and you'd have been calling me Red. Thanks."

He'd brought a woven straw hat and her beach robe, and he was clad in slacks and kamehameha shirt, and when he said abruptly, "Better let me do your shoulders," she submitted as docilely as though she'd known him for years.

"You do have a name, or do you?" she asked.

"Oh, yes, two of them. Which would you prefer, the one I was christened or the one by which loving little Lakeville knows me?"

"Both," Sue answered.

"I was christened James Edward Weaver. Lakeville's loving ones call me 'that good for nothing beachcomber.' I'm called Ed by my friends."

"Hi, Ed."

"Hi, Sue."

Sue stepped into the canoe with the deft balance of an expert, then slid down to the cushions. "Nice combing," she remarked.

Weaver's hand made a quick move to his hair, blond hair with a tight wave, and Sue laughed.

"I mean beach combing—the trophies. Oh, you even remembered my sandals."

She pulled on the sandals, pulled the floppy hat over her now dry hair, draped the beach coat over her shoulders and sighed with contentment. "This I like."

Weaver nodded. "Only one thing missing— food. That's across the lake. Have you time to go over?"

She nodded. Why not?

"Then pull that robe over your knees or tomorrow you'll be saying your prayers standing up."

They talked of foolish inconsequential things as he sent the canoe flying to the eastern shore of the lake; then abruptly he said, "Sue, you haven't asked me a single question."

"I'm on vacation."

"What has that to do with it? Susan, what do you do when you're working?"

She laughed up at him. "Don't tell me you don't know? Really? I run an employment agency, a clearing house for loggers." Her voice faltered. Ed Weaver had lifted his paddle and was looking at her with consternation.

"Sue, I didn't know. Does your aunt realize what you're doing?"

"What's wrong with it?"

"You don't understand. Nothing, nothing at all; it's grand. But how a girl like you, looking like something out of a finishing school—"

"Some finishing schools allow a modicum of intelligence," she reproved.

And then she wondered what had possessed her to come out alone with a man she didn't know, a man who admitted Lakeville called him a beachcomber. And she felt again that queer little chill of apprehension.

"You'll think I'm crazy, Sue, but I wish you'd promise me something. And believe me, I've never been more serious. Don't let anyone know what you've been doing."

"But why?"

Again he sat, paddle held up, crystal drops sliding off to plop into the lake. He seemed to be weighing what he would tell her, or was he weighing her, her intelligence?

"Lakeville," he said at length, "is a vicious little burg." He paddled a few strokes then spoke again. "Sometimes it's better to let people underrate your wisdom. It throws them off guard. They show their hand sooner."

Then swiftly he sent the canoe on to the shore where low buildings were sheltered under wide oaks and where other oaks leaned over the water to provide a cool cavern for canoes.

They had hamburgers and iced coffee served to them in the canoe, and Weaver talked of the settlement springing up among the oaks. "Mostly young couples. Not much money, but they have a wonderful time."

"No keeping up with the Joneses?"

"They've found the easy way to avoid that—community picnics in the summer, no-host parties in the winter. And without bitter competition for show."

19

A voice came from the bank above. "Hey, Weaver, your logs are in."

"Great!" Weaver's answer boomed back. "See you this evening."

Sue said she must return; her aunt would be worried about her.

"Especially," she laughed ruefully, "if she should find my car at the beach and no signs of me swimming."

"She'll know where you are." Weaver spoke with confidence. "Everybody will by sundown. No, I'm not being a Tom. This is just by way of warning."

Sue frowned. "How do they do it, by radar?"

"No, the evil eye." He was half laughing. "Now let's see how long it takes you to identify that."

He told her he wanted to see her again; that he was not welcome at the house, "not at present. But somehow I have a hunch, if you're the girl I think you are, there's a change coming."

He turned in to the least crowded end of the now busy beach, and when she thanked him for everything he smiled. "This is the first happy day I've had since I arrived."

"Then why do you stay?" Sue asked.

"Because I'm a stubborn man," he burred. "I refuse to be run out. Be seeing you."

Sue drove into the old stable and, walking out the garden side, found the earth saturated with water, the garden drenched. The heavy purple cups of canterbury bells lay half filled with mud;

colored stars of nicotinnia were crushed under some earlier play of water.

And then Sue saw her aunt. Mrs. Cantrell was playing the hose full force without any sense of direction, now here, now there, her attention indrawn, only the nervous movement of her hands indicating her mental state.

"Aunt Lovey—"

The hose was dropped and Lovenia Cantrell came ploughing over plants to reach her niece. "Susan, Susan, why did you do it? That terrible man. And I'd counted on you. I'd thought, if Susan ever reaches here she'd find a way."

Sue started to draw her aunt to the little summerhouse, then saw the sodden condition of her clothes and propelled her on to the big house. "Find a way to what, Aunt Lovey?" she asked.

Chapter Three

Lovenia remembered the hose, and Sue ran back to turn off the hydrant, and when she returned her aunt seemed more composed. She had removed her wet clothing and donned a cotton housecoat and sat plucking at the folds.

"Aunt Lovey, tell me what is bothering you? Why are you so distraught?"

21

"I can't tell you, Sue, because I don't know. I haven't a thing in the world to worry about, not really, yet . . . Susan," she leaned forward to whisper as though the house were crowded with enemies, "I'm losing my mind."

"Of course you are," Sue began.

"You musn't say that. Milly scolds me when I even mention it. She says it's dangerous to believe you're becoming incompetent."

"Will you let me finish? You are your mind, Aunt Lovey, and you're wandering around lost in forest of bugaboos. As for you worrying, thinking you're mentally incompetent, that is the one sure sign you're not."

"You mean?"

"Dear, haven't you heard it's the people who need a psychiatrist who never accept his service voluntarily? They are positive they are right and all of the rest of the world wrong."

Mrs. Cantrell sat up. She nodded; then the frown returned to her face. "But the other women —Today I heard one dear friend say, Poor old Lovey's really slipping."

" 'Dear friend'?" inquired Sue angrily. "Well, next time flash back, 'Of course I am; I'm trying to get down to your level.' "

"Then you really don't—"

Sue stood before her aunt, a small, determined figure. "Look, sweet. From what you said of this small town, all one has to do is start a rumor and it becomes a fact. Some place you have unwittingly stepped upon someone's toes. They've struck at you to get even. They've perhaps said your mind wasn't as good as it once was. By the time that thought had gone the rounds the last gossip had you ready for the State home.

"Now what are you going to do, sit back meekly and let yourself be railroaded by gossip, or be yourself, the quick-witted Lovenia Cantrell?"

Lovenia Cantrell stood up, throwing her shoulders back as though ridding them of a burden. "Right now," she quipped, "we're both going to dress, or had you forgotten our dinner engagement?"

She brushed her tan-colored hair until it looked like freshly pulled taffy, and then she wasted moments choosing the right frock and, laughing, finally selected a shrimp pink linen because that was the only color that didn't make her skin look parboiled.

As she came downstairs she found her aunt cutting off the end of a belt to her print dress. "Sue, you look adorable," she said, and began pinning the loose end. "I'm still wearing the same old things. Intended making them over, I've lost so much weight."

"Maybe we can make up some new things," Sue interposed. "Aunt Lovey, shouldn't you tell me something about the Macks?"

Mrs. Cantrell settled her belt in place, then nursed a pricked finger. "Well, there's Milly, and

Melvin, who's not a Mack but her brother. She's terribly fond of him—raised him, you know."

"And Mr. Mack?"

"Oh, he died quite some time ago, before they moved here. And then there's cousin Hetty. I don't see how Milly puts up with the poor old woman, but that's Milly. Wait, isn't that their car? Didn't you hear—"

"I did," said Sue, "but I don't answer car honks. There's plenty of parking room." And then she stopped because of the expression of her aunt's face. "It's just," she concluded lamely, "that I don't like to be treated like a poor relation."

Mrs. Cantrell had hurried to the door; now she looked back. "Come on, Sue; Milly's with him. Hurry, dear."

Sue moved forward on obstinate feet, thinking with each deliberate step. I-am-not-going-to-like-Milly-Mack.

But she did. Milly was coming up the walk as Sue stepped through the door, and Sue was completely unprepared for warm friendliness of the woman. Or her appearance. She'd anticipated someone large and pompous, but Milly Mack wasn't large, and unless you could imagine a blackbird being pompous, she wasn't.

Her eyes were deep and dark and her hair so purely white you thought for a moment it must be a wig. And the grey silk slack suit she wore pointed up the whiteness of it. Slack suit?

"Susan dear, you're going to have to get used to

24

our country ways. She does look shocked, doesn't she, Lovey? Lovey, you look so cool in that print. But let's hurry; I threw things at the stove and left poor Hettie to watch them.

"Melvin dear . . . Sue, this is my brother Mel. Suppose you ride up there with him."

Sue barely saw Melvin as he walked her around the car. He was a little taller than she and very compact, that much she knew. And he had a low pleasant voice. "Sis rather sweeps one along, doesn't she?" he asked, his voice indulgent.

She looked at him then and found he had a way of bending his head and looking sideways as though inviting one to share some secret amusement. And she saw his eyes were blue, his lashes very thick and sunbleached at their tips, just as his hair seemed sunbleached from crown to brow.

As soon as they left the tree-shaded street the late sun still burned warm on their shoulders, but Melvin turned the car toward the lake, and what was called "the evening breeze" relieved the heat.

"We like to have dinner just at sunset," Milly was saying. "The view from our terrace is so beautiful. But this daylight saving time——"

Dimly Sue heard her, for just as she hadn't been prepared for Milly, she was totally unprepared for Seefar. Lovenia Cantrell had written of the Mack estate. But she hadn't said the estate was a vast ranch, that there was fifteen minutes of rapid driving between the big rock arch entrance and the house.

"Our land begins here," Melvin Roth had remarked, just as he'd commented upon different landmarks along the way.

And then when they topped a rise and a further hill crowned by a mass of buildings came into view, he said, "That's the house."

A moment later he said, "Congratulations," and when Sue breathed a question, answered, "You didn't say, 'Why did you build way out here?'"

"Are those who ask penalized?"

"Oh no, but it's refreshing to find someone appreciative. Actually the original building was here when Milly . . . when it came into Milly's possession. But wait, don't look back. I want you to catch the view with one deep breath."

He circled the hilltop, pulled into an enclosed driveway, saying the wind could be severe at times, then with an explanatory, "It's my turn," to Milly, led Sue through a glass door to the terrace.

She drew the one deep breath. The view was stupendous. It was even greater and more all-encompassing than that which Sue had seen as she was driving into Lakeville.

For miles in every direction were hills, but the hills which had looked barren at midday were now bathed in the rosy orange of the setting sun, their folds deep blue and purple shadows.

"That's Lakeville, just below."

Lakeville lay in the shadow, a dark pincushion

covered with the sequins of street lights, the long lake a mere shadow beside it.

"Melvin," Milly's voice came from the house, "dear, will you roll the table out? We must have dinner before it's time for lights. Bugs *will* appear from somewhere."

Mrs. Cantrell came out then to stand beside her niece. "What do you think of it?" she asked eagerly.

"Beyond belief," Sue murmured.

"Too much sky," her aunt commented.

Not for Sue that night; the sky was part of the glamour of the evening. She could imagine the winter sunsets when the sky was green and orange and the hills covered with snow, but she was satisfied with this night as it was.

The dinner was simple but tasty, and for tables they used individual benches which could be rolled up or away so no one need be cheated of the view.

There were a few lights in the house behind them, but these were soft and didn't compete with the stars which swung lower and lower as night deepened.

Sue met Cousin Hettie. She was to meet her several times before the old woman's personality made any impression upon her, for Hettie's appearance, her voice and her personality were all monotone.

Melvin went into the shadows to "check on our man," Lovenia and Cousin Hettie to wash the dishes, and if a slight question appeared in Susan's mind as to why such an establishment didn't carry a staff of servants, it was quickly brushed away by Milly.

"We cherish our privacy," she explained, "and so few servants will live so far from town."

And then she laid a slim hand on Sue's arm and said in a soft, confiding voice, "Dear, I'm so glad you've come to Lakeville. You're going to spend a few days, aren't you?"

"Probably a few weeks," Sue confessed.

"Wonderful. I've been so worried about Lovey. Tell me how do you think she looks? Being with her almost daily, it's difficult for me to judge."

Sue considered this a moment. "She doesn't seem physically ill, but she has changed."

The hand tightened on her arm. "I know. She's probably told you I'd like her to come up here and live with me. As you can see, we've worlds of room. But she will cling to her past. And, Sue, I worry myself frantic over her down there alone. Almost anything could happen to her."

"Oh?" Sue's voice was dreamy. "Then why hasn't it? I mean, she's been living there for years."

"Yes, dear, but her husband was with her. Now she's completely alone. Oh well, I'll have a nice mental vacation while you're with her. I'm sure you're capable. You work in some office, don't you? Clerical work, I think Lovey said."

Sue sat up with every intention of telling of her position, but just then a searchlight flashed along

28

the lake, and she thought of the lake and what Ed Weaver had said and answered only, "Well, yes, clerical." For there was clerical work connected with it.

Later, after she was home and on the very edge of sleep, she reviewed their conversation and was surprised that she could have been so influenced by a man like Ed Weaver.

She knew more about him now. As soon as their home door had closed behind them her aunt had sighed deeply. "Milly is terribly distressed at you going out with Ed Weaver today."

"I didn't *go* out with him, Aunt Lovey. As I told you before, I swam further than I realized and he had the good sense to realize it."

And then she grew curious. Weaver had told her everyone would know exactly what they had done.

"How did Milly know?"

"I suppose someone telephoned her. Everyone in town knows how close we are. And they'd know you were my niece. As Milly says, there's no damage done and I must not scold you, since you didn't know the man nor what he is."

"What is he?"

"He pretends to be a writer, but no one has ever seen anything he's written and no one can see how he can accomplish anything; he's always on the beach or hanging around some bar or cafe in town. Writers have to work."

Sue nodded; she'd known a few. "But, Aunt

Lovey, much of their work is done mentally before it's put down on paper. Maybe he's gathering material."

"Milly said if you stood up for him you were only defending yourself and I musn't blame you."

"Oh, darn Milly," moaned Sue. "I'm tired."

Her aunt stood at the newel post as Sue started up the stairs. "Sue, dear, just one more minute. This town—well, it's one place where you can't run with the hounds and hide with the hares. You must belong to one side or the other. This Weaver—"

Sue had a sudden suspicion. Was Milly Mack the head of one faction and Ed Weaver of the other?

"He belongs to neither side. He's just a trouble maker. Considering the way he lives, a veritable beachcomber, you wonder anyone pays any attention to him."

But they do, Sue thought. She had. However, as she'd said to her aunt, "I doubt I'll ever see him again; he said he wasn't welcome here."

She didn't see him for two weeks, the busiest two weeks she'd ever enjoyed. They were one round of parties.

Milly Mack gave a tea for her and from that moment on she was entertained from morning until midnight. Swims, breakfast barbecues, luncheons, teas, dinners, evening barbecues.

Sue didn't know how long this might have gone on, had there not come a morning when she found her aunt on the kitchen floor in a dead faint and, unable to reach the physician she'd met socially, called another, a Doctor Foster.

He was brusque and unfriendly until Lovenia Cantrell, regaining consciousness, took one look at him and fainted again.

"Poor soul," he said. And to Sue, "It's a mental condition, you know."

"You mean some mania?"

"In a sense. Worry is sapping her." He stopped.

Sue pondered. What had her aunt to worry about? She said as much, and the doctor shook his head at her. "Someone told me you were exceptionally intelligent. Could they be wrong?"

He wrote a prescription and told her to which drugstore to take it. "So she'll know she's not being poisoned." Then he said, "And call Doctor Devaux; she trusts him."

He was at the door when he turned back to add, "And don't let *anyone* take her away from home to nurse her."

When Sue went back her aunt was lying, eyes wide with fright. "What is it, Sue; what's wrong with me?"

"Nervous exhaustion, Aunt Lovey; you're going around carrying some burden of worry. You needn't. I'm here to take over."

For a moment hope burned in the wide grey eyes; then they blurred with tears. "You don't know—oh, you don't know," she sobbed.

She was quieting when the telephone rang, and

as Sue turned to answer it, she grabbed Sue's hand. "Promise me, Sue, promise me that I can stay right here in my own bed. Promise, Sue."

Sue patted her. "I've already promised the doctor. Don't worry; I can be tough."

It was Milly on the telephone asking what was wrong. She'd heard that awful Doctor Something-or-other had called. Had Lovey had a stroke?

"Goodness, no," said Sue. "Nothing but nerves, worry."

"Susan, you're trying to shield your aunt. I want the truth. I know she's had a stroke. I'm sending my own physician, and then we'll call an ambulance and have her brought up here. You can't take care of her alone. Here we can relay, with Hettie and myself, and Melvin's also very good. Now I'll—"

"Please *don't*," Sue managed to make herself heard. "It's nothing serious. Aunt Lovey merely fainted." Sue heard a noise and looked around. Her aunt was standing at the study door. "She's already up. A few days' rest—"

Sue helped her aunt back to bed and stood frowning down at her. There was so much she didn't understand, and this wasn't the time to discuss it. "Is there some neighobr you'd like to have in while I go to the drugstore?" she asked.

"No, no one. If you have anyone in they'd answer the door. If you just lock up when you leave I won't be disturbed."

"I won't be long."

The druggist said the prescription would take a few moments to fill, long enough, Sue decided, to have a cold drink. She went to the soda fountain to stare blindly into the mirror, directly opposite.

Frosted across the big glass were prices: sundaes twenty-eight cents; malted milks, thirty-five; and then between the price of sodas and milk shakes she saw the face of Ed Weaver, watching her.

Her response to his smile was quick, involuntary.

"May I sit beside you?" he asked, and when she nodded, moved up. "Is your aunt feeling better?"

Sue looked at him in mock horror. "Do they have a town crier?" she asked.

"Alexander Bell did away with those. No, I just chanced to overhear a conversation on a street corner. I'd been wanting to meet you off the reserve, so when one woman said to the other that you'd been seen flying out to the car with a slip of paper she thought was a prescription, I hied myself into the only drugstore your aunt would patronize."

Sue shook her head in wonder. "They didn't tell you what was the matter with Aunt Lovey, did they?"

"No, but they did say Milly Mack was coming in to take over, that you'd refused to move your aunt out there. That's why I dared hover in your vicinity."

Sue jumped off the stool. "I'll have to get back."

And then she paused. "Don't you ever swim any more?"

"Yes. How about the drink you ordered? Aren't you going to take it? You can, you know. You locked up before you left."

This time Sue leaned weakly against the stool. "Talk about living in a fish bowl. It isn't that I mind anyone seeing anything I do, yet—"

Slowly the blond head nodded and the blue eyes were bright in the deeply tanned face. "Privacy. We all like it. Sue, I'm going to hand you a slip of paper. A map. If you will, meet me there. I'll have the canoe. Say nine-thirty tomorrow night?"

Sue's eyes were level with the blue of Ed Weaver's shirt. She stared at it a moment, saw it stretched tightly across his broad chest and felt an utterly insane desire to lean her head against it, beachcomber or no beachcomber.

"I can't promise," she evaded, and then belligerently, "but I will try."

"Good enough. I'm leaving right now. I won't even pick up your check. It will be better for you."

And he was gone. Through the mirror she watched him stride easily along the crowded aisle, saw the sun flash on his hair as he reached the street; then he was gone.

A few moments later she was hurrying out to her car, annoyance and distrust of Milly Mack fighting with logic. Hadn't her aunt said Weaver stirred up trouble? Of course her aunt had been determined she wouldn't go to the Mack house, and it was thoughtful of Milly to come down to help, yet—

She raced to the house and was foolishly relieved to find her aunt all right, no one trying to break down the doors, not even the telephone ringing.

"What is that medicine?" Lovenia demanded.

"Just a sedative, sleeping pills. Why?"

"They'll really make me sleep? How long?"

"Goodness, Aunt Lovey, I don't know. Several hours, I imagine. Why?"

"I want to go up to my own room. It's cooler. Come, let's go right away. I'm all right; I'm not weak."

She was strides ahead of the shorter Sue. True, she clasped the railing grimly and mounted step by step, but once in the upper hall she all but flew to the southeast bedroom.

"I don't wonder you prefer this," Sue remarked, as she hurried to put fresh linen on the bed, find a silk coverlet, and plumped up pillows. "There's an actual breeze."

"Hurry, let me have the pill. The doctor said I wasn't to be disturbed, didn't he? Didn't he, Sue?"

"Yes, and no one will disturb you. Not up here."

Lovenia Cantrell lay back on the pillows, cheeks white but a look of triumph in her grey eyes.

35

"Not up here," she agreed. "Milly is afraid of stairs. Milly's husband was killed, falling downstairs. She won't have any in her house."

Chapter Four

Sue went to her own room to straighten it before returning to kitchen duties. She moved slowly, thoughtfully. Was it possible her aunt's friends were right? That she was becoming mentally ill?

Sue had just started washing the breakfast dishes when Milly and Melvin came to the rear door, their arms loaded. "Brought you a few things you might need," Milly announced. "It's so difficult to cook for an invalid, and Hettie began whipping things up the moment I told her about Lovey."

She lay covered dishes and pans on the table and ordered Melvin to place his in the refrigerator, then return to the car. "I'll run right in and see Lovey."

Sue had to follow her to check her rush to the den. "She's asleep," she began, and to Milly's "I'll just peek," added, "upstairs, in her own room."

"Upstairs!" Milly turned a face tragic with remembered horror and Sue knew a desire to shake her aunt.

"It's so much cooler," she hastened to explain. "The big black walnut shades it from the south, and if there's a breeze it comes in from the lake through the east windows."

She found herself babbling in her effort to atone for some shock she'd given Milly, Milly who had hurried to help a friend and been slapped for her effort.

"But she must be brought down." Milly had recovered. "The dining room is cool. Melvin can telephone for help and move the furniture some place, then bring in a bed."

"Milly, please listen. Aunt Lovey isn't actually ill."

"She's in bed, isn't she? You can't run up and down those dangerous stairs twenty times a day. Suppose you slipped and she was sleeping or didn't hear you. No, she must be brought right down. Melvin—"

Sue turned to Melvin, who was looking at her with that sidelong glance of amusement. "You might as well give in," he advised. "When Sis is in one of her Florence Nightingale moods nothing will stop her."

"Florence Nightingale wouldn't disturb a patient who'd been ordered to sleep," Sue said, laughing, "and I'm afraid that heavy furniture couldn't be moved without a great deal of noise."

Milly stood tapping her teeth with a fingernail, then turned to her brother. "Melvin, Sue's tired, or will be before the day is over. You run up and look in on Milly. Now tiptoe; be as quiet as you can." She turned to Sue. "She hasn't had lunch, has she? Then, Melvin, take up the beef aspic. I'm positive Lovey doesn't eat enough proteins. Now where were we?"

She wheeled suddenly and went into the dining room, and Melvin laughed. "Those two. I don't know which is the more determined. Sis thinks up an idea and tries to put it over, and Lovey gets busy and slides out from under. I'll bet she moved upstairs on purpose, didn't she, Sue?"

Sue felt relieved. Of course it was no more than a battle of personalities, but she was still Lovey's niece. "On purpose to sleep in comfort." she said. "That den is like a desert at midday. Are you going up?"

He returned to assure his sister that Lovey was sleeping. Yes, he'd tiptoed over to the bed. No, she wasn't breathing in rasping gasps. Yes, she had some color in her face.

"It's fine up there, cool," he reported, and Sue felt he was pouring oil on very troubled waters.

They left soon after that, Milly giving a final warning on the danger of stairs. Sue returned to cooling dishwater, talking to herself. "I will *not* fall down those stairs," she said angrily. "Great goodness, if Milly could see those steep crazy stairs at the mill, she'd have cause to throw a fit. But didn't I run up those and down as well, twenty times a day? Me and a hundred men?"

Sue fell downstairs that night.

Lovenia had awakened at twilight, rested and hungry and declaring if Sue could stand the extra work, she, Lovenia, intended to "remain in that room for a week" and just rest. "There's no sense recovering too soon," she reasoned, "and if I'm here I won't have to answer the telephone and explain why I don't want to be on the go every moment of the day."

Going on to her room, Sue realized Lovenia hadn't once said, "Milly thinks," though unquestionably Milly didn't approve of wasting one's time reading mysteries. Lovenia was obviously having a rest from her perennial duel with her friend.

Sue turned her mind then to her own problem. With her aunt so much better, she could meet Ed Weaver the next night. She laughed a little, because slipping out after dark seemed so silly. Yet it would be nice to make a move without everyone knowing about it.

She turned off her bed lamp and stretched, aware of surprising weariness. Of course she'd gone up and downstairs. "Now there I go," she scolded herself. She'd made no more trips than she was accustomed to make on other stairs.

It was then the telephone rang. "Darn," said Sue. She fumbled for the light, for her slippers and her robe, then as the insistent clamor went on started to run, and failed to turn on the top light.

She missed the first step and panic swooped down in like a smothering blanket. Panic. She named it and instantly relaxed to roll on down like a puppy.

For a moment she lay in a crumpled heap at the foot of the stairs, aware of intense pain in her right ankle. Then the telephone, which had stopped for the moment, began again.

The lights flashed on and above her Lovenia Cantrell looked down. "What happened?" she asked in a frightened voice.

"I got smart and tried to slide down the banister. Oh, that phone?"

"Susan! Wait. If that's Milly, don't you dare tell her you fell!"

It was Milly, an anxious Milly. What had kept her so long? Was she all right? She was? Then was anything wrong with Lovey?

"I couldn't find the light switch," Sue lied cheerfully. "And of course I couldn't find my robe."

She listened to a dissertation on the proper placing of robe and slippers, should there ever be a fire, and then Susan asked if there was some special reason she had called?

"I only wanted to make sure you were all right before I retired."

Sue looked down at her swelling ankle. "Fine. Aunt Lovey was able to eat a fair dinner. Shall I report in tomorrow morning?"

"What a peculiar term, report in. Well, goodnight, dear; I'd better call you."

Sue made a painful way back to the stairs to find her aunt tripping down. "I bought five pounds of Epsom salts, especially for this," Lovenia announced, "and an elastic ankle brace. Now sit down while I locate them. Thank goodness the foot bath is upstairs."

She looked at her aunt and began to laugh, and then Lovenia sat down on the bottom step beside her and joined in.

"Would you mind telling me how you knew I was going to fall," Sue demanded, "before you even knew I was coming to visit?"

Lovenia wouldn't talk until they were back upstairs and Sue's foot was immersed in a hot Epsom salts bath.

"Someone *had* to fall," she explained; "that's why I moved downstairs. I didn't mind getting hurt, or even getting killed, but I simply would not let Milly say, 'Now what did I tell you?' "

"Why did someone *have* to fall?"

"Haven't you noticed if you're warned against a thing you begin to anticipate it? Your muscles tense, and when they do you lose the firmness of your step."

"Well, for goodness sakes," cried Sue, "that's why I was so tired tonight. I have been tensing. Milly kept warning me, and I kept tensing against her warning until—"

"You preferred the banister to the steps?" teased her aunt. "Move your foot; I'll put in some hot water."

Sue looked thoughtful. "Aunt Lovey, you really don't like Milly Mack, do you?"

41

"No, Sue, I don't like her. I love her, but I don't like what she does to me, in all kindness."

Lovenia helped Sue to bed, arranged pillows to ease the ankle and even threatened to bring one of her own sleeping pills, but Sue insisted she could sleep.

Sue had planned to have a long talk with her aunt the next day. But that had to be deferred. Her ankle was still badly swollen and woefully painful. It was Lovenia who slipped downstairs to do such work as needed doing, and Sue who sat on the front porch, slack suit covering the bad ankle.

Neighbors came in a steady stream. They brought everything from a whipped cream cake to a book of crossword puzzles. Lovenia was back in bed, and a few went up to look at her and convince themselves, and others, that her niece had reported her condition accurately. The poor darling was only tired out.

Milly telephoned that she wouldn't be in, and Sue walked to the telephone like a martyr to the stake, and the watching visitor didn't know of the damaged ankle.

But she knew she couldn't slip out to go canoeing. And suddenly it seemed terribly important that she should. She insisted to herself that it was only because the day had been so hot that she was thinking of the canoeing, of dark waters buoyantly below and stars overhead and music coming across the water.

"Dear child, are you in that much pain?"

Sue looked up at her aunt. "Not physical. But I had counted on slipping out when you weren't watching to go canoeing with the beachcomber."

"You were? Why Susan—" Lovenia's voice took a sudden drop. "Well, why not? Is he expecting you?"

Susan's mouth opened a time or two before she could overcome her surprise enough to reply, "sort of. I wasn't sure. I saw him yesterday when I went in for your prescription."

"And there's no way to get word to him. Hmmm," buzzed Lovenia; then she tossed her head. "What's to keep me from sliding out in the dark and telling him why you couldn't come?"

She did. She put on a dark dress, picked up a scarf and, with the air of an adventuress, scurried through the shrubbery to watch for a break in headlights of cars on the lake shore.

She tried to read, but when the expected half-hour stretched to an hour she felt frantic that she couldn't at least get up and pace the floor. And when the telephone rang she almost ran to it.

But it was Milly with her goodnight call. "I thought I'd call before you went upstairs," she said, and Sue wondered how she could know where she'd been when the telephone rang. "Those stairs, you know. I'd hate to think of you hurrying down, tripping and falling. So dangerous."

"Aren't they?" agreed Sue, and Milly went happily on to say she would be away the next couple of days. She had to make a trip to the county seat, on business. Sue and Lovenia must be good girls in the meantime.

"We'll try." Sue all but wept, for where was the delinquent?

Lovenia Cantrell came in within the next half-hour. "Did you worry? I just forgot all about the time. My, it was wonderful. The music and everything."

"Music? Aunt Lovenia, are you feeling all right?"

"Oh yes! That reminds me, I must get some dishes and spoons ready, and that whipped cream cake. Do you think you'd like coffee as well?"

"As well as what?" asked Sue guardedly.

"As ice cream. He went into town for some.

"He?"

"The man I went canoeing with, Sue, the man you sent me out to meet. My, it was lovely, with the stars and the little waves when the breeze came up. I don't know when I've had such a good time. Mmm, must pull the blinds."

Sue swam up from the depths of her amused shock to ask why. "No one can see in here."

"They can see the lights, can't they? A person doesn't sit in the living room alone for any length of time, not in this house. They would know you had company and become curious."

And then she gave a little jerk and started for the kitchen.

Lights, mused Sue. She'd wondered how Milly knew she hadn't gone upstairs.

Lovenia came in with a tray, coffee service and cups to say, "One night I forgot to turn the light off in the bathroom. Milly had a fit. She said, aside from the waste of power, she'd suffered, thinking I'd had a stroke."

Sue stirred angrily. There was that stroke again. "If she was so worried, why didn't she come down to investigate? Or she could have called someone who was closer, whoever it was told her about the light."

"Oh, I think I hear him." And Lovenia was bustling to the shrub-shaded north door.

Ed Weaver stalked in hardly glancing at Sue's face, his attention focused on her ankle. "Let's have a look," he said, and added, "good evening Susan."

She yelped a few times as he probed, but he paid no attention until he sat back on the ottoman he'd drawn up and nodded. "Hold everything; you're not going to like this. Mrs. Cantrell, stand behind her and hook your hands under her arms. Now, ready?"

When he was through he handed her a fresh handkerchief to mop her face and remarked to her aunt that they'd have to eat her ice cream, he doubted she'd want any. Then he said it was a darned shame a private citizen couldn't call a doctor without having to explain to everyone in town.

"You'll be all right now," he promised. "We'll

give you a couple of aspirins, and I'd better carry you up to your room."

"You don't need to," Sue interrupted. "Aunt Lovey," she added with seeming irrelevance, "Milly called. She's going to be away for a couple of days."

Mrs. Cantrell looked from one to the other, then said brightly, "Oh, did I tell you? Sue turned her ankle in the garden *tomorrow* morning."

"And you heard her call, tomorrow morning," Ed took up the story, "and felt so much better you decided you didn't need to remain in bed. Which will free you to answer the telephone so they won't have the marines in to effect a landing."

"So we can make up a bed right here on the divan," concluded Mrs. Cantrell. "My goodness, that coffee has been perking for twenty minutes."

Ed Weaver couldn't stay; he was meeting the midnight bus. She didn't care. All she wanted at the moment was some relief from the steady throbbing in her ankle, an ankle which seemed to have extended its area of pain to her very shoulders.

"Thanks so much for setting it," she said.

He made two flying trips up and downstairs, bringing Sue's bedclothes, pillow and the book she'd intended to read. And watching his free easy step on the stairway, Sue felt confidence returning.

"If you need me at any time, put a green reading lamp in the east windows of your room. Sorry I can't telephone. We have a privately owned telephone system here."

Mrs. Cantrell offered her hand. "Come back, young man. Any time you can, come back."

Ed Weaver looked at her steadily. "You don't really mean that," he told her. "It's all right. I understand."

For two days Sue and her aunt lived in semi-retirement. Without Milly to supervise, they could avoid calling a doctor who would instantly have said the injury was more than a few hours old. "Just a bad strain," Lovenia told the inquiring neighbors.

Milly Mack returned on the third day. She drove directly to the Cantrell house, so filled with news Sue's ankle received blessedly scant attention.

Milly followed Lovenia to the kitchen and Sue missed the first part of the story, but Lovenia had coffee ready and Milly followed her back in, still talking. "The town was simply agog, Lovey. Here was the poor young veteran searching for his wife, and she'd simply vanished.

"I didn't pay too much attention until I heard the name Ed Weaver; then naturally I asked for the details.

"It seemed this veteran had gone on a short trip, he didn't say where, business I assume, and when he returned his wife was gone, even her clothing, everything that she could legally call her own.

"He seemed to be suspicious of some man, and when he was told his wife had taken a Lakeville

47

bus he just shouted, 'Ed Weaver. She's gone to him.' "

Milly paused to look triumphantly from one to the other, and Sue was thinking, the Lakeville bus. Ed Weaver had said he couldn't stay that night because he was meeting the midnight bus.

"Someone," Milly continued, "told him I was from Lakeville, so when he asked if we'd room for him to drive back with us I naturally said we had. It's little enough we can do for these boys who're facing such horrors. And of course on the way up he told me the whole story."

A quick movement caught Sue's eye. Lovenia had jerked in a peculiar fashion. Milly was unaware of it. She went on, "It seems this poor man, Ladue, went down to some military hospital for a check-up. He was away several days, and when he returned he found his wife gone.

"Someone, some woman from Lakeville, had seen her up here, and she right up and told the man his wife was running around with Ed Weaver. He was furious, naturally. His wife came home, and he admits he really beat her up and she —now imagine this—instead of going to the police she telephoned Weaver, and he, mind you, threatened to horsewhip Ladue. Did you ever hear of such a thing?

"Well, anyhow, Ladue was so upset he and his wife began to quarrel, and after one bad quarrel she simply disappeared. So he got in touch with this Lakeville woman and discovered she'd run off up here to join Weaver and was with him now.

"Ladue says he won't stop until he *gets* the man who stole his wife."

Milly stopped, and again Sue saw her aunt jerk.

"Did you give him a gun, Milly?" she asked.

"Lovenia Cantrell!"

"Aunt Lovey!"

"It would be such a simple way to rid Lakeville of an unwanted presence," Lovenia explained innocently. "The wronged husband would be exonerated, wouldn't he?"

Chapter Five

Sue leaned back on the divan cushions. Her mind and her heart were in turmoil. Aunt Lovey definitely did need the services of a psychiatrist. And Ed Weaver. Well, what had she expected? Goodness knew he'd never treated her as though he thought her more than a tool he could use to hurt someone, to cause dissension.

"My dear," the warm pressure of Milly's hand on Sue's, "you must not hold it against me that I was the one to tear the scales from your eyes."

She left then, and Lovenia, after seeing her to

the door and waiting until the car was out of sight, came back to look down at Sue.

"Milly is going to send Mel back, with the car. We're going up there."

"Aunt Lovey, I definitely am not!"

"It's cool on their north terrace."

"I wouldn't care if this was Arizona in August."

"Susan, please. For my sake. I'll tell you everything later. I'll bring down a light dress; those slacks must be warm."

For a long moment they stared at each other; then Sue relented. What did it matter where she was just now?

Lovenia brought the most demure-looking frock Sue possessed, a pale green organdy.

"Like a lime sherbet," Lovenia told her, appearing herself in a faded paisley print of voile.

Mel was there by the time they were ready, Sue walking with the aid of a cane which had once belonged to Ned.

"Blistering, isn't it?" he said unnecessarily. And after they were in the car, "Lovey, Anne telephoned. She has to go into town for something. Milly said you wouldn't mind sitting with her mother. I'll come back for you later."

Sue waited. Why, if this Anne had wanted a mother-sitter, hadn't she called Lovenia? And was her aunt going to have her services disposed of in such a manner?

She was. Don't bother coming back, Mel; the drive isn't worth it. I'll go on home."

They let her off at a small cottage, then drove on, and Mel said, "Sis is sort of a clearing house for the Women's Club. She's the kind women confide in, you know. They're always bringing her their troubles, so she knows who's available and who isn't."

They sped along the lakeside, and the sun reflected from the water was dazzling to the eyes. And Mel said, "Sue, do you realize this is the first time we've ever been alone together?"

She looked at him quickly. "Why, I guess it is. I hadn't thought—"

"I had, but as fast as I make plans something happens to destroy them. Sue, how about evenings; couldn't I come down?"

Again Sue looked at him, this time in surprise. "Why not?" she asked.

"We could send Lovey to a movie. Sue, I'm so sick of talking to you through a half-dozen other persons. Do you realize I know nothing of you? Just the scraps I picked up at parties. They're not enough."

"There's not much to know," she told him.

"You really don't have any close relations, except Lovey? And you really have to work, Sue? You shouldn't, not anyone as lovely as you. Working coarsens girls."

He had slowed the car, and the sun beat down, and Sue was still ill from the shock of the morning. "Couldn't we drive a little faster? It's so terribly hot and I'm not accustomed to it."

"Of course. Just one more terribly important question, Sue. Are you engaged? Oh, I know you're not wearing a ring but is there anyone special, any understanding?"

Sue brought up a laugh. "Dozens of specials and dozens of understandings. Or do you think I sit at home and dream?"

"Hardly that," he said, "but I had to know."

They'd passed the steep pillars and were going up the steep winding hill. And then they pulled up behind the buildings.

Sue caught a glimpse of Milly, pacing the north terrace. Then she approached the car to greet them.

"Of course you know I trumped up a reason to keep Lovely in town," Milly confided. "Melvin, bring us some iced tea, will you, dear?"

At least she was open about it, thought Sue.

"I've never had a real heart-to-heart talk with you. There was always the danger of Lovey interrupting. And, Sue, I'm worried sick about Lovey, not just her physical condition but . . . Susan, do I dare tell you what I think?"

Sue braced herself for what was coming.

"Her mind, had you noticed?" She waited a moment, then said, "But it wouldn't be right for you to comment. Loyalty to an aunt, and of course any mental disorder would reflect upon you."

"Not necessarily," Sue interposed. "Only certain types of mental disorders are inherited."

Milly looked at her quickly, then spoke again.

"Of course it's her financial condition. Has she discussed any business matters with you? Sue, I know this sounds terribly personal, but I do have the right to question."

"You mean the right of friendship?"

"That, and something more. Lovey, you know, owes me several thousand dollars."

Now Sue knew the bottom of her world had dropped out from under her. With one part of her mind in a state of shock, the other was asking, but how could she? Where is there any evidence of her aunt using anything but the strictest economy?

"Dear, now don't let this worry you. I'm not pressing her for payment of any kind. But you know it's a proven fact that when one is indebted to a friend, one begins to hate instead of love that friend. And I'm terribly afraid Lovey is beginning to hate me; that this hate is part of her mental disturbance."

"I wouldn't know," Sue said helplessly.

"And of course you're not in a position to help her, while I am. If she'd only *let* me. Oh, here's Mel with the tea."

She wondered if even the cool mint-flavored tea could pass the constriction in her throat. Several thousand dollars. And to think she, Sue Thompson, had thought *she* could help her aunt.

Melvin drank his tea thirstily, standing, then carried his glass away and disappeared.

"So many of Lovey's friends have noticed the change in her." Milly set her glass down on the table beside her and began pounding her palm with her fist. "Sue, we have to work fast, or it will be necessary to put her away!"

Put her away. Put her away. The words made a chant. Sue sat stiff with shock. She couldn't meet the waiting, probing gaze of Milly Mack, so she looked out and down and saw the long narrow end of the lake curving around a low hill.

And all of the words she would have spoken were pushed back. Regardless of what Ed Weaver was, he had given her good advice. She wasn't ready to fight for her cause, not yet, so she would seemingly agree.

"What can I do?" she asked.

"Well, now," there was the triumph of a point gained in Milly's voice, "with your help we can plan to protect her. The first thing, of course, is to sell that awful house of hers."

Sue sensed, rather than saw, a movement in the shrubbery behind Milly. Milly was intent upon a notebook she'd drawn from an inner pocket, intent upon the figures she was scribbling.

"Now if she'll sell the house—"

It *was* a figure behind the shrubbery. It was Cousin Hettie, and she was staring at Sue and slowly shaking her head.

"She would have enough to pay me. Not that I mind the debt, except that Lovey is feeling it to the point of hating me. Then she could clear up her indebtedness around town, and then by mov-

54

ing out here have plenty in the bank to keep her the rest of her life."

"But would you want a crazy woman living with you?" Sue asked.

"Crazy? Dear, you haven't understood. But then you're so terribly young and inexperienced. Once Lovey's mind is free of care it will become normal."

There was more. Sue dimly heard it. She had too much to think about and wanted none of it revealed on her face.

"When you're ready to leave it will be time enough to discuss this with Lovey. You still have a job, haven't you? Which reminds me, how is it possible for you take such a long leave of absence?"

"My office is in the extreme fire hazard district serving logging operations. It always closes down this time of the year."

"Naturally. Well," Milly sighed happily and stood up, "you rest here, dear. I have a tremendous amount of work to do. Yesterday, while at the county seat, I discovered a most underhanded dastardly plot against the taxpayers of Lakeville. It must be stopped. So you'll excuse me if I do a little telephoning?"

Sue held the "Gladly" which came to her lips and substituted, "Surely." She even looked up as Milly laid a warm hand on her shoulder, and believed nothing of what she was feeling showed.

And then she lay looking out on the world,

looking at the folds of hills merging into the sky, their outline smudged with summer haze. Her world was smudged, too. No matter where or how she looked at it, there was no distinct outline.

She wished she could leave, but now, like Lovey, she had learned to be wary. She could hear Milly's voice, not the words but the accented demand of it, as she telephoned.

And suddenly Sue lifted her head and smiled. Why, of course. The reason she herself had questioned her aunt's sanity had been Lovenia's attitude toward Milly Mack, her words. Well, if Lovenia Cantrell, because of this, was ready for a psychiatric ward, she could move over and make room for her niece. Sue Thompson agreed with her.

The sky grew hazier, a shadow curtain before thunderheads piling up along the far mountain tops, and Sue wanted to go home now more than ever. She should always drive her own car; then she could leave when she was ready.

Cousin Hettie came out on the terrace. "I got supper 'bout ready. Guess you want to freshen up. No need you walkin' clear to the ell; you come with me."

There seemed to be an urgency about her and Sue responded. They went through a tiny hall which led to the kitchen and then to the service area, and here Hettie held open a door to a small bathroom, obviously her own. "No need to make much noise," she advised, "nor stay long."

For a moment Sue looked at odd things in the small room that spoke of Hettie: the wooden-backed brush, the old-fashioned hair oil, a nainsook nightgown, well patched.

And then she was aware of a window and something moving outside. Softly she stepped to a vantage point and looked out.

She saw a high hedge boxed around a space no more than six feet square. In the center was a stool and on it was Melvin Roth. He had a notebook on a small table beside him and was making rapid notes without lookin at them. He couldn't; he was busy looking through a telescope.

Sue stared at the telescope. It was a powerful instrument, mounted on a strong stand, the end of it protruding through the hedge.

And suddenly Sue understood. She understood how Milly could tell when the people in the Cantrell house retired, when a strange doctor's car drove up before it, when a visiting niece went canoeing with a beachcomber.

She recalled a telescope in the forestry lookout near her office. It wasn't half the size of this, but the rangers could look at a big clock on a building sixty miles away and tell the time. With this telescope Milly Mack could keep track of the movements of half, if not all of the people in nearby Lakeville.

Ed Weaver had known of this. He had said, "I wonder how long it's going to take you to identify the evil eye."

Chapter Six

Quickly Sue slipped out of the little room. She found Cousin Hettie waiting at a turn in the hall, listening, Sue knew, to Milly, still at the telephone. She pressed the old woman's hand reassuringly, added a pat of gratitude and was back on the chaisette when Milly came out a few moments later.

Dinner was served almost immediately. The thunder heads were higher, a grey film spreading to the zenith, and sheet lightning was revealing the form of lower, angry clouds.

"I should be getting back," Sue said.

"No, dear, you're staying tonight, I've already telephoned Lovey."

Sue remained quiet. She wanted to scream. She wanted to tear down some invisible wall which was closing around her.

"Mel has chores to do with this storm coming, and I know you wouldn't want him to neglect them when we have so much room."

Sue stood up, groping for the cane. "Then I shall call a cab."

"Why, Susan," Milly Mack was smiling, but

there was a peculiar look in her eyes, "one would think—"

She thought quickly. What possible excuse could she make that would free her from this place? She realized that from now on, until Aunt Lovey was free, it would be a battle of wits between her and Milly Mack.

Sue's quick glance swept the room. She knew now what lay behind much of Milly Mack's mania for power. She would play upon that.

"I'm sorry," she said, "but you know how it is. I'm sure your mother ingrained certain rules of conduct in you, things one simply doesn't do? And aren't they terribly hard to eradicate even when you know the modern world isn't so particular?"

It worked. Milly could remember any number of foolish notions, yet she could understand. Mel would take her home. If he hurried there would be time for the chores.

The wind was blowing in gusts when they left; its vacuum was like gasps in-drawn, sucking the car to one side of the road, then pushing it to the other.

But Mel seemed to revel in it. He laughed a great deal. "Sue, Sue, you're wonderful," was all he said, but he said it so often she wondered what he meant. And when she asked why he answered, "You look so innocent. You look, my lovely, so dumb. And you aren't."

The first big drops were falling as they ran up

the walk to the door. The porch light was on and Sue saw Mel's blue eyes gleaming with a wild light.

"When Milly calls, tell her I'm taking to cover until the storm is over," he said and, laughing, ran down the walk and jumped into the car.

"Sue," Lovenia drew her into the hall, "Milly telephoned early that you were spending the night. Sue, you didn't quarrel with her?"

"No, darling. Not after the showdown we had. I thought fast and told her it wasn't *comme il faut*. Nicely bred girls don't spend the night without their accoutrements."

Lovenia had closed the door and was pulling her more deeply into the house. She waited for a peal of thunder, then asked tremulously, "Showdown? What do you mean, Susan?"

"*She* showed," Sue replied, and then she turned to Lovenia. "Aunt Lovey, Milly Mack is the most dangerous person I've ever met."

"Sue, I wonder if you realize how really dangerous she is."

"I don't know. I know enough to want to guard every word and every act. And I think part of her danger lies in the fact that she believes she's a public benefactor. She completely and honestly believes what she does is right for the person for whom she does it.

"Aunt Lovey," she said suddenly, "run up and turn on my bed lamp and the reading lamp in your room which shines out on the catalpa tree."

60

Mrs. Cantrell looked at her a moment, then nodded. "So that's how she does it."

"I'll turn off this light and you use a flash. She won't realize then that we are holding a conference; she'll think each of us is in bed, reading."

Left alone in the dark, Sue sat watching the rain, silvered by a street lamp, running down the window pane. She thought of Cousin Hettie and wondered what fires were banked behind the ash grey of her demeanor. And she thought of Mel and his wild, triumphant laughter.

"Freedom," she said aloud. "He knew he was going to have a few moments of freedom. The storm was too severe for anyone to sit outside and watch the headlights when they left here, to sit and trace them. Our living room light would make her think he'd remained here until the storm was over."

She wondered vaguely where he had gone, where he could go in a community so closely knit every person's every move was accounted for.

And she wondered how long after the living room light went out, for that could be seen without the eye, Milly would call and ask about Melvin.

It was half an hour. She warned her aunt not to answer too quickly, that she was supposed to be in her room. "And, Aunt Lovey, let her think Melvin came in for a moment."

By that time Lovenia was ready to do anything

Sue suggested, for they were having their long delayed talk.

It had started when Mrs. Cantrell came down from turning on the lights. "Tell me everything," Sue had said. "Don't spare yourself, because if I am to help, I must know."

But now that Milly had called, Sue felt they should go upstairs, prepare for bed, turn out her light first, then later the one in Lovenia's bedroom.

"It sounds silly," Sue confessed, "but if Mel acts as he sounded, he won't be home tonight and Milly may start out to trace him. She'd stop here first. And if she found us talking, she'd know she hadn't psychologized me into believing what she said this afternoon. She must believe that."

They went back to a resume of what had been said earlier. "So there I was," Lovenia said, "with that great stack of debts, the hospital bills, though actually I had borrowed on our property to pay those, the funeral bills and all of the accumulation of little bills which had piled up during those long months after our income stopped.

"Ned's insurance didn't begin to take care of them. I went to the bank thinking I could refinance, but the bank refused because I had no visible means of meeting the payments.

"Then I tried other means.

"I was at the end of my rope when Milly came in one day. I hadn't known her too well; Ned didn't care for her. But she seemed, I thought then, to sense what was wrong, and before I was really aware of what had happened, she had refinanced for me so I had enough to pay off everything, and enough to live on for a little while.

"You can imagine the depth of my gratitude."

Sue nodded. She knew how stricken she'd been at the death of her father, and he'd left no debts and had left enough to see her through business college and to buy an annuity.

"I wouldn't have accepted even that," Lovenia continued, "but I was positive I could find work. Other women older than I were holding positions I could fill. I would find something.

"I didn't, Sue. Several times I was hired, but before I could go to work I would receive a call that the position was no longer open, or that they were sorry, someone had hired someone else earlier. All manner of excuses.

"Sue, I thought there was something wrong with me."

Sue looked at her with interest. "What do you think now?"

"I always hurried to tell Milly about the new job. Now I know she got in touch with whoever was in power and told them, oh, one thing or another. I'm not sure what, perhaps something different each time."

They were silent a moment, listening to the thrum of the rain, and then Sue asked, "How do you stand now?"

"Milly holds a mortgage of thirty-five hundred

seventy-nine dollars and seventy-nine cents. I have three hundred left, not enough to see me through the winter."

"Any current bills?"

"A few, none of great importance. I've been holding back because I felt if I failed to make payment to Milly every month, she would foreclose as a *loving gesture* of taking care of me. In short, forcing me to live with her."

"Aunt Lovey, do you know why she wants you?"

Sue could see the silhouette of the nodding head. "A man can't run a kingdom alone. She must have those around her upon whom she can depend, completely. She believes dependence is assured through fear."

"Fear." There was something not clear there. With the property sold, and surely it was worth several thousand, Lovenia would have been independent. She wouldn't have become a grey ghost haunting the outer fringes of the Macks' life, as Cousin Hettie was.

"Well, darling, we'll sleep on it. And don't worry. I have over two thousand in savings. We can live through the winter on that, Milly or no Milly. And I have a feeling we'll find a way to clear up everything."

"Sue, I can't use your money."

Sue patted her hand. "Now don't worry. I doubt if we'll have to. You'll probably be lending me money before we're through with this. 'Night, dear, and tonight, sleep."

Sue and her aunt awakened to a world that looked as though it had been washed, starched and pressed with a shining iron.

Lovenia sang as she prepared breakfast. "I'm starved," she broke off to say once. "I feel as though I'd been living on husks for years. Sue, do look in the fruit closet and see if there's any grape jelly left."

She must rush through some canning. She hadn't had the heart to do anything before. "I couldn't look forward," she said, "but now I can. Oh, Susan"—she turned to her niece—"if we could only find some way for you to stay on here. You need a real home and I need you."

"We'll manage something," Sue promised.

A neighbor came over with a loaf of hot bread and gossip. "Out to my brother's ranch when the storm started, so we sat it out. Didn't start home until 'long about three o'clock this morning. Well, sir, we were driving along peaceful as you please when this car came a-roaring down the road behind us. Like to pushed us into the ditch. And who do you think it was?"

Lovenia and Sue expressed complete ignorance.

"Melvin Roth," the neighbor brought up in triumph. "Musta been over to the junction. We come upon him later on; he'd pull off the side o' the road to fix something. Bob stopped and asked could he help, but Mel said, no, wasn't anything much."

The telephone rang soon after the neighbor left. Lovenia answered and called Sue. "It's Milly; she wants to talk to you."

Sue went to the telephone with great reluctance and stiffened to apprehension when she heard Milly's voice. Oh, it was pleasant and confiding, but it was thick with reproof.

"Dear, your insistence upon going home last night could have caused poor Melvin's death. His car broke down halfway home and he had to sit out in that storm, lightning flashing all around him. He didn't come in until ten o'clock, three hours after he'd delivered you. Of course I doctored him and put him to bed, but, Sue—"

Sue stared at the telephone. Why was Milly lying? Some reason lay behind it. Why? Because it was necessary for her to have a scapegoat? No, it was because Sue had won out last night. She had to destroy that victory.

"You'll remember, Milly, I wanted to take a cab and you wouldn't let me."

"Of course I wouldn't." Milly's voice was like a whiplash. "You couldn't afford a cab. No one knows that better than I. Sue, I want to have a talk with you."

Sue turned from the telephone and fear coursed through her and she could understand her aunt. How could you win against a liar?

She went thoughtfully about her work. Milly could have lied about Ed Weaver as easily, if it served her purpose. Though of course others had seen him meet this girl, drive away with her. Nothing more had been heard of the vengeance-bound husband.

Sue spent the day going through her aunt's papers. There weren't many. Most of them were in Milly's safe, as Milly had said a fire could quickly destroy an old frame dwelling so she'd take care of them.

"She has the deed because she holds the mortgage," Lovenia explained, "and of course the insurance papers. But I do have the copies."

And Sue could find nothing that would give Milly such an assurance of power over her aunt.

Evening seemed forever coming. For once Sue thoroughly detested daylight-saving time. It stretched the hours to the point of breaking, she thought.

And then twilight came and Sue draped an emerald green scarf over a reading lamp, pulled the blinds on the north side, leaving only the east window open to the lake.

It was amazing how quickly Ed Weaver responded. Sue, letting him in at the side door, felt such relief she was faint.

"I was expecting it," he said. "The old gal has been on a rampage all day. I couldn't think you'd be unmolested."

"But it wasn't today," Sue told him. "I'd have

signaled last night except for the storm and the fact I knew she was looking for Melvin."

They stood in the dark back hall like two conspirators, and Sue told him her findings. "But there is something more, something I can't isolate. Do you know anyone at the county seat who can check on Aunt Lovenia's property, at the court house?"

"Yes," he said thoughtfully. "I can't phone from here. I'll run into Junction City right away, then wait for the return call. It will be afternoon before I return. Now how can I get the information to you if you should need it in a hurry?"

Lightly Sue touched his arm. "Ed, I found it, the thing you called the evil eye."

"Good Lord, how!" he ejaculated, and as quickly, "Does she know?"

"No. The person who let me see it is the last who'd want her to know."

"The old lady. Incidentally, I found out by accident. A forest ranger spotted the sun shining on the lens and was curious, so he had the air patrol check. As their station is a hundred and fifty miles from here and they thought it nothing but a plaything for some idle rich, nothing was said, locally."

He left, saying he would find some way to get in touch with her. And he did, the next afternoon.

A gypsy came around selling willow garden chairs and, finding Sue alone, gave her an envelope. Inside she found a message that made her sink into the nearest chair.

No taxes or assessments have been paid for two years. Amount totals $835.79. Advise immediate payment in person. Property due for sale Sept. 10.

Chapter Seven

Lovenia Cantrell, coming into Sue's room, looked at her niece and cried, "Dear, you're white as a sheet. What's wrong?"

"Nothing that can't be corrected," Sue answered. "Sit down while I hurl questions at you, Now, how do you pay your taxes and where?"

"Why, Milly pays them. She said she'd feel safer about me if she took care of it, indicating of course that I was so absent-minded—"

"But doesn't the county assessor send the notices to you?"

"She arranged that by having them sent to her address. Lots of absent owners have their notices sent to their residence, a different address. But why, Sue?"

Sue sighed. "I'm getting out of here as of now.

Oh, why didn't I put all of my money in a checking account?"

And then she told her aunt what Ed Weaver had found. "I'll have to drive to Timberton, draw out my money, then go on to the county seat and pay this off. I want to see those papers cleared. And of course there will be a penalty, so that must be taken care of at the same time."

"But, Sue, you can't leave now. Milly telephoned. She is giving a command party tonight; full moon stuff. You have to be there."

Sue looked up in apprehension. "What's up this time? Milly never gives a big party without some reason, and that reason's not the pleasure of her friends."

"For once we're not involved. I'd better give you the whole picture."

Lovenia sat down near Sue and began, "I'm seeing things so differently now, Sue, seeing both sides instead of just Milly's:

"Lakeville hasn't always been as vicious a little town as this. Of course all small towns seem worse because everybody knows everybody's business and new gets around faster. People are closer together and their native antipathies aren't insulated by the indifference of the city.

"And everyone in Lakeville does not dance to Milly's whistle. As you've noticed, the town is more or less divided.

"With the newcomers and their families, Milly's opposition has grown. These young couples and others object to our schools. The buildings are inadequate. Teachers receive their appointments by favor instead of ability.

"There is a special election due. Three board members are up for re-election.

"The opposition is putting up three to replace the originals. And they are trying to float a bond issue to rebuild two of the schools."

Sue suddenly remembered her last visit to Milly, the few words she'd heard as Milly concentrated upon telephone calls and Milly's remark that she had, while at the county seat, "discovered a most dastardly, underhanded plot against the taxpayers of Lakeville."

Lovenia needn't have said more. Sue knew the program. Milly would gather her trustees about her; with them would be those who faltered on the outer edge. But after having been entertained at the fabulous Milly Mack home, how could they help but put their shoulder to the wheel that would crush the opposition?

Underhanded. But one had to be underhanded to break even with Milly. She worked so silently and swiftly one was tied up before becoming aware of it. Look at the condition of Aunt Milly's property.

"And I don't know that's all she's done."

It was the not knowing what to expect that forced one to work in the dark, literally to sneak behind Milly Mack's back.

"Sue, you can't make that long drive with a bad ankle."

71

"I must. My problem is how to explain my absence."

She had no right to call on Ed Weaver, and even though she were driven to it, she couldn't this night, with Milly's command dinner party to attend.

She was nearing the point of desperation when her aunt called her downstairs. The gypsy was back, white teeth gleaming as he held up an atrocious fern stand. "Here you are, lady; I made it just like you wanted. Two dollars, for you I make it; for other people five." And then one beautiful eye was covered by a long-lashed eyelid.

"Cheap at half the price," breathed Sue. "Will you wait until I get some change?"

She carried the light basket stand to the veranda and with it the concealed note. In the hall she read it. "If you will trust me with your plans I will try to help. Learned mortgage is really deed of trust with provision one payment overdue allows foreclosure. You can beat this risk by having outside bank handle payments."

It took Sue a moment to digest this. Then she understood. A bank in which Milly Mack was a controlling stockholder might mislay a check long enough for proceedings to be started. Certified checks from an outside of the area bank could not be mislaid.

Swiftly Sue wrote her answer. "Will leave for Timberton immediately after party tonight. Thank you for everything. P.S. If you learn anything more in the meantime slip a note under the north door."

Sue dressed for the party feeling she was strung on tight wires, that anyone touching any part of her would set the whole jiggling.

"My, you look pretty," Lovenia groaned when Sue came to her room. "I swear my fingers are all thumbs. Sue, how am I going to go through with this party tonight?"

Sue wished she had the answer, but she must not let her aunt know how she felt. "Have a grand time, darling. Pretend as you've never pretended before. And yes Milly every time you have the chance. Here, you're hooked up wrong, and you'd better let me do your hair."

She hooked the dress, then snapped her fingers. "Dear, Mother's amethysts are perfect for this dress. Why didn't I think of them before? And I'll sweep your hair up like a dowager duchess."

Lovenia Cantrell stared at herself in the mirror. She couldn't believe it. She didn't look like a thoroughly whipped old woman about to exist upon charity. She looked no more than her middle age, charming, competent, wonderful. Something within responded and her head lifted proudly.

Sue's dipped. Milly would see the change; however, if this would carry Lovey through this trying evening Milly would only blame it on Lovey's niece. And that was safer for Lovey.

"Milly's going to be so busy putting over her

program she won't have time to pay attention to us," Sue prophesied.

Milly Mack would be very busy, but Mrs. Cantrell and Miss Thompson had been ordered to appear early. Milly's quick glance swept Lovenia and darted to Sue.

"Doesn't she look nice?" Sue asked. "I wanted her to do you proud."

Sue was watching Milly as she spoke, and she saw the long fingers curve and felt the woman longed to destroy the smart coiffure, to rip off the amethysts, to turn Lovenia back to the drab person she'd made of her.

"Dear," she whispered to Sue, "I want you to be especially nice to Melvin tonight. Something happened to him when he took you home in that storm, and he hasn't been himself. You weren't unkind to him, were you?"

Sue widened her eyes. "Why should I be?" she asked.

Milly squeezed her shoulders. "You're an asset to any party," she murmured. "Now, Lovey, if you will help Cousin Hettie, and, Sue, you might put on an apron and begin."

Sue, trying to keep pace with Milly, looked over the preparations and thought anyone would enjoy one of Milly's parties, regardless of whether or not they liked Milly.

There was the long buffet, with the silvery white of linen a background for adroitly arranged food; platters of meat cold and hot, shining aspics of green and crimson, mounds and bowls of salads, massed prawns on beds of shaved ice, tureens of dressing, condiments beyond counting. And later there would be steaming casseroles.

Just as later the overhead lights on the terrace would be extinguished and shaded candles offer no competition to the stars overhead and the glitter of street lights below.

"How does she do it without servants?" Sue whispered to her aunt.

"Organizes her efforts," Lovenia whispered back. "She makes her plan, fits it to her time and lets nothing interfere."

The guests were arriving. Sue found herself standing beside Milly, acting actually as co-hostess and very puzzled as to how it happened.

Yet she enjoyed it. And then she saw Cousin Hettie coming toward her, Cousin Hettie dressed in a becoming grey voile. "I'm to relieve you," she said: "Milly wants you a moment. She's in the living room."

Sue relinquished her place at the coffee urns and went across the terrace, stopping now and again to speak to someone about a party to come or one she had missed, to answer questions about her aunt's health or her own injured ankle.

Milly grabbed her wrist as she came through the door, and Sue felt some intense disturbance run from the hand to her arm.

"Sue, I'm frantic. It's Melvin."

"But I haven't seen him all evening."

"Of course you haven't. He's sulking. We had a terrible scene just before you came. He's in the sun room. Sue, do go in and see if you can't get him to come out. It's so embarrassing. Everyone's asking about him."

"I'll see what I can do," Sue said doubtfully, and found herself pushed to the inner sunroom door.

Melvin was there. Sue's first glimpse caught him sitting in a straight chair, his head dropped forward, his hands clasped and hanging loose between his knees, a picture of utter dejection.

"Mel"—she spoke softly, pity for him thick in her voice "am I intruding?"

He jumped up quickly, looked at her squarely and said, "Please, Sue, for your own sake, go away."

"For my sake? From the hill, do you mean?"

A change came over him then. "It's no use," he said in such a low tone she could hardly make out the words. "No, don't go. I have to talk to you, Sue. I *have* to, understand?"

She wondered if he had been drinking. She wondered at the look of anguish in his eyes, something which said he had been goaded beyond endurance.

"But I don't understand."

"Sue, it's you. I love you. There's nothing false about that; I do love you, Susan. I have since the first time I saw you, but what chance did I have with you?"

He'd come close now, gripped her wrists, and words were pouring out. "What am I to win you?" And again, "Sue, you have to say yes. Sue, it's the only thing that can save me."

Save him from what? But he was talking rapidly now, breathing heavily, his eyes bright with eagerness. "Once we're married we can get away. It's the only way. Once we're man and wife, once there are two of us . . . Oh, Susan, you will?"

His arms were about her, holding her tight against her own frantic resistance.

And a bright light came on, the side door to the terrace was thrown open and Milly Mack's voice cried, "Why, *here* they are. *Melvin! Sue!* Oh, my darlings, how wonderful."

She babbled on, the chorus of laughter and congratulations from the guests overriding her voice, and Sue waited, frozen with embarrassment.

She saw faces, but only two were clear; her aunt's, filled with horror, and the face of Cousin Hettie. And Cousin Hettie was signaling.

"Sue," Melvin's voice was a threat now, "play up. Don't you dare let Milly down before her guests. *Don't you dare.*"

Chapter Eight

The Sue Thompson who had come to Lakeville two months ago would have acted promptly, vigorously. But that Sue had never lived in a place like Lakeville. She had never known a woman like Milly Mack.

This Sue Thompson had learned caution. She saw the need for caution in the gesture of Cousin Hettie, nodding her head and tapping her ring finger. And she saw it in the alarm on the face of her aunt, an alarm which asked nothing for herself.

So Sue smiled, a smile so innocent it brought a deep sigh of relief from Melvin, of triumph from Milly.

A beautiful ring was brought forth by Milly. "My very own," she said softly, "the one my husband put on my finger when I was even younger than you, Sue."

Sue looked at the ring and felt the circle of platinum a trap, the great gleaming stone an eye as evil as the one hidden in the shrubbery.

"Here, Mel, you put it on," Milly ordered.

But Sue held her hands locked behind her. "It's

too beautiful," she said. "Besides, I'm terribly superstitious about such things."

"Susan!" She had to meet Milly's eyes, and she wondered how much the woman could see in her gaze. And she thought desperately, I can't let her give it to me here before all of these witnesses. I must throw back her challenge before them.

"If you really love me, Milly," she said, her voice soft, "you won't ask me to go against a family tradition, you who believe so strongly in traditions."

She'd won. For the moment.

"Well, of course, dear, if you feel that way." And she turned to Melvin. "You must find something equally fine for Sue. Of course this was a little unexpected."

Sue had only a vague idea of what went on after this scene. Melvin was attentive. He laughed too much and too loud. He brought heaping plates for both and both left them untouched.

Sue was aware of chairs being assembled in something resembling a ring, and then Mr. Foss, the bank manager, began discussing the petition the malcontents were getting up, and the need to defeat the move.

There were others who spoke. But Milly, never. And Sue gave her credit for the deepest wisdom. Milly never fought in the open. She had too many in her dominion to fight her battles.

The party broke up early. Someone said they must arise early, and Milly said of course, it was thoughtless of her to invite them in the middle of the week, but hadn't the moonrise been worth it?

Sue didn't even know the moon had risen.

Neither Sue nor her aunt spoke until they had driven through the stone arched gateway; then Lovenia said, "Sue, why is Milly trying to force you to marry Melvin?"

Sue gave a rueful laugh. "She isn't, Aunt Lovey. I think she planned to give me an engagement ring that would disappear. The engagement would then be broken and I would be called upon to pay for the ring. I couldn't, you know, not without taking every cent I have."

"So that's why you refused it. I was cudgeling my brains to remember any family tradition. Sue," her voice became more alert, "then why is Milly trying to—"

"Frame me?" Sue supplied the word. "Because she realizes I'm not as dumb as I look."

"But how does—"

"Thanks for the compliment, darling. I think the gal is tops in extra-sensory perception. She senses the change in you and blames me. She needs you. I think she knows Cousin Hettie has reached the point where she's going to revolt. Mel is showing signs of rebellion. She's having to tighten her controls."

"Then Mel doesn't—"

Sue drew up at the old stable entrance. "I think Milly threw me as a sop to Mel. He sees in me a way to break free of Milly. Aunt Lovey, I would like to know how Milly got such complete control over Mel."

They didn't speak again until they were in the house; Sue went to the north door entrance and swooped upon an envelope. She might have known she could count on Ed Weaver, but not this far.

"Auntie, everything's all right. I'll be home tomorrow night."

"How can you?"

Sue had hurried away from her and was now pulling a telegram from the mail box, taking the hanging notice of it from the front door.

"And here's something you can show Milly. It's supposedly from my boss. Listen. 'The I.R. claims discrepancy in first quarter report. Unable to locate your carbons. Am sending plane to Junction City for your convenience. Please come immediately. C. A. Mott.' "

"Who's the I.R.?"

"Could be Internal Revenue."

"Sue, is this real? Then suppose Milly decides to telephone this Mr. Mott?"

"I'll be there before the call comes in. Now to dash."

Sue didn't turn on her headlights until she reached the main thoroughfare. At the city hall she checked her mileage, and two and a half miles further on came upon the scene she expected, a car supposedly broken down.

She slowed and Ed Weaver came up to her.

"Move over and I'll drive; give us a chance to talk. I phoned a friend in Timberton while I was in Junction City arranging for the plane. He knew your boss and arranged the wire."

"That was such a relief. But about the plane, you chartered it?"

"Not exactly; belongs to a friend of mine. You can pay for the gas if it will make you feel better. Stan considers it a privilege to have an excuse for flying. About tomorrow: you will have to wait until the bank opens; then Stan will pick you up and you should make the county seat by two o'clock. Stan will plan to be back at Junction City soon after dark. As long as you're not expected it will be safe to drive on in from there."

"Safe? What do you mean?"

He slowed the car to a crawl and Sue was aware of a night wind sweet with dry grass, aware of the strong hands on the wheel, the shadows cast upward by the dial board lights.

"I don't know, Susan. Because I don't, I shouldn't say things to frighten you. I shouldn't have warned you in the first place. You'd have been better off dancing around as one of Milly's satellites."

"You might give me credit for some judgment. I'd have been wary of her without any prompting from you. I was apprehensive before I even reached Lakeville. At that," she conceded, "I think I learned more quickly because you warned me not to let her know I wasn't subnormal."

A string of colored lights appeared ahead, and again the car slowed. "I didn't have any dinner," Ed said. "Suppose I bring us out some hamburgers and coffee."

"Wonderful," said Sue, and hid her laughter. Hamburgers and coffee after the food she hadn't been able to eat at Milly's party.

They sat in companionable silence for a few moments, then Sue asked, "What I can't understand is why Milly is so obsessed about Aunt Lovey. Considering Milly's wealth, why bother with such a drop in the bucket as Aunt Lovey's home?"

If she could pick that up for a thirty-five hundred dollar mortgage and sell it for twenty thousand, its natural price, that isn't chicken feed. Well, I'll take these cups in, then get on our way."

When he came out he drove with some speed and very little was said. Sue had noticed a car following them, and called his attention to it. He said, "Mine. You'll be better off if you're not seen with me."

They topped a rise and a wide valley lay below, airport beacons to the north of the little town.

"I'll get out here." He stopped the car and waited while Sue slid under the wheel, and she was aware of the other car pulling up a little ahead.

"Sue"—he stood beside the car, his face grave —"I'd give almost anything if I could take this whole thing out of your hands, take care of everything for you. But I happened to get involved in another matter at the wrong time."

Sue saw a movement around the other car. A girl had stepped out and was walking around in front of the headlights. She was tall and dark and strikingly beautiful, in a scarlet sweater and skirt with a wide band of scarlet tied about her hair, a vivid note in the night.

"Involved"—Sue's voice was husky with hysteria—"you think *you're* involved. Ed, tonight *I* became engaged to Melvin Roth!"

She was in gear and now shot the car away from him, away from his command to wait.

Sue had made one flight in an air-liner, but that was totally unlike this small plane Ed Weaver had arranged to carry her on her mission. She liked the pilot Stan Burry. He was plump and jolly and had the air of setting forth on a lark.

It might have been one for her except she could not erase the memory of the tall vivid girl from her mind. Ed might at least have introduced them, she thought resentfully, then remembered she had pulled away rapidly.

In the air, with dawn filtering in, she did remember what he'd said, "I'd give almost anything —" and then thought that could have been nothing more than the natural desire of a man to protect a girl. Besides, wasn't she engaged to Melvin Roth?

They came down into the practically deserted Timberton and Sue went directly to the hotel, leaving a nine o'clock call. Even three hours' rest, after the tension of the previous day and night, was something.

Slipping into bed, she thought she had never felt so completely dejected. She had gone to Lakeville thinking she might help her aunt, and instead had become so deeply involved she couldn't see her way out.

"Oh, why not be honest about it?" she said aloud. "You're in love with Ed Weaver and haven't a chance with him."

She slept then and, awakening from deep slumber, let the bell ring a few times before she could orient herself. A cold shower and breakfast did much to revive her spirits, to bring hope like a reluctant sun to the horizon of her life.

When the bank opened she was there and quickly transferred her money to a checking account and, with a letter to a county seat banker from the local manager, hurried back to the plane.

Now the sun was blazing down and she alternately dozed and worried. Two thousand dollars had seemed such a lot of money when she'd thought of it as something to fall back on in case of illness, or between jobs. But two thousand dollars applied to Lovenia Cantrell's problem was a mere drop in the bucket.

She spent nearly half of it before she again boarded the plane for Junction City.

Sue squirmed around in the seat of the light

plane until Stan looked back, worried. She gave him a smile and went on with her problem.

How could she and her aunt continue to live on what was left of her savings? Especially with the problem of heating for the severe Lakeville winters? And the monthly payments to Milly?

The plane circled Junction City field and Sue drew a deep breath. Well, here she nosed back down into her troubles.

As they came in she scanned the parking area for cars. There was her small car and—her breath caught—there was the Mack car.

For all of a moment she was ready to beg Stan Burry to take to the air again. She couldn't, simply couldn't face Milly Mack right now.

Melvin was waiting for her, and this posed a fresh problem of how to pay for the trip. Then she thought swiftly and said to Stan, "Mr. Mott gave me the money for the gas; will you please give me a receipt so I can mail it back to him?"

And then she turned to Melvin. "What on earth are you doing here?"

Before the flood lights were turned off she caught a clear look at his face. It seemed grey, lifeless, and then the darkness swept in and he appeared more normal.

"Milly told me to pick you up, said you'd be too tired to drive home."

"But my car's here, Mel."

"We'll drive back for it after you've rested."

"How did she know when I'd return?"

"She didn't actually. She telephoned the Timberton hotel and they said you'd checked out, so she reasoned you'd be in sometime today."

"I might have stayed at the camp, you know."

"She thought of that and telephoned the airport. They said your plane took off at ten-thirty this morning, so she told me to come here and wait until you showed."

Sue had heard of people seething. She thought she'd been angry before, but she knew she'd never felt such fighting anger before, felt as though she must strike physically to relieve the tremendous pressure building up within her.

"What business had she telephoning around the country to check on my whereabouts?" she demanded angrily.

"She needs you, Sue."

"*Needs* me?"

"We found Cousin Hettie dead this morning."

When Sue could speak she whispered a question, "Dead?"

"Suicide. She left a note. But can't you imagine what this has done to Sis? Let's hurry. I'll stop and telephone we're on the way."

Chapter Nine

Melvin steered Sue to the car and helped her in, then went back to the office to put in a call to Lakeville. And as he went in, Stan Burry came out.

"Note from Ed," he reported quietly. "His car will follow you back. He says to tell you this, whatever he means, is a reprieve."

Some of the sickening fear left Sue then. She felt less numb when she reached for the receipt.

Melvin returned and reported Milly greatly relieved. "She's worried every minute since she heard you were flying. She said you should have called us and let me drive you there."

"That would have taken two days, Mel, and," there was no hesitancy as she continued, "the matter couldn't wait." Let him think she referred to Mr. Mott.

They were out of town and near the top of the grade before either spoke again. Sue, seeing a car where she had seen Ed's car another night, spoke to draw Melvin's attention from it.

"Tell me about Cousin Hettie," she said.

Melvin drew a deep breath. "I helped her clear up last night after the party. She was washing dishes when I went to bed, so we don't know what time she turned in. This morning Milly waited for her coffee, rang a couple of times, then went looking for her."

Sue shivered.

"She went into her room and Hettie seemed to be sleeping, comfortable position and everything. Sis went over to shake her and . . . well, she wasn't exactly sleeping."

"But how, Mel—what was it? Did she have a bad heart or what?"

"I told you it was suicide." His voice was edged with anger. "She left a note. All right then, she took sleeping pills, deliberately."

"The note—" Sue heard another car behind and relaxed a little.

"She actually left two, one to whomever it may concern, and one to you."

"To me!" cried Sue. "But, Melvin, she hardly knew me. We couldn't have exchanged more than a dozen words."

"Yeah, I know; that's what has us puzzled." He slowed the car and spoke irritably. "That car's trailing us. I'm going to let him pass."

"Wouldn't it be better to hurry?" she asked, "if Milly's waiting? Mel, what was in the note to me?"

"Well, she left you something. She said you weren't to wear it but just keep it as a reminder. It was a ring."

Sue's breath caught in her throat. A ring as a reminder. She'd meant as a warning. Well, at least that established the fact that Hettie's death had been suicide.

"Sue, why don't you say something?"

"I'm puzzled. A ring for a re . . . oh, of course, she meant to remind me of her. The poor darling, didn't she have any people of her own, Mel? I know you called her cousin, but—"

Mel had heaved a great sigh when Sue explained the reminder. "That had Sis puzzled, too, but of course that's what she meant. She took quite a fancy to you, I think. She said once you reminded her of a little girl she'd nursed and tried to adopt. No, she didn't have anyone. She was just one of Milly's waifs."

Just one of Milly's waifs. Sue filed that thought away for future consideration.

Melvin went on talking. Milly was giving Cousin Hettie a quiet funeral; she had no friends around Lakeville. Milly didn't believe in "putting on a show at a time like this."

He referred to the car behind them several times, speeding, then slowing, until finally Sue said, "For goodness sake, Mel, whoever it is wants to reach Lakeville just as we do. There isn't any other road."

The car turned off on the first road after they'd reached the Lakeville outskirts, and Mel shortly turned the other way.

"Your aunt's at the house with Milly. Milly sent me for both of you as soon as she found Cousin Hettie."

Sue braced herself for the meeting with Milly. As they made the last curve she could see Milly's silhouette pace back and forth, then come to a waiting stillness as they approached.

"For you to have run away just when I needed you—" was Milly's greeting.

"If you want to call it running away. Where's Aunt Lovey?"

"She's worn out. She's been taking the telephone calls for me today, so I simply made her lie down. She's in Cousin Hettie's room."

Sue turned back, her eyes blazing. "How could you? Knowing Aunt Lovey, how could you? It's like making her step into her shoes."

"Oh, for pity sakes, Sue, don't be absurd."

Melvin stepped in then. "She's not being absurd, Sis; you wouldn't lie down in there. I know you."

She whirled on him, and Sue rushed on through the kitchen to the remembered room across from the little bath.

Lovenia Cantrell wasn't lying down. She was sitting erect, her jaw set, such a look of indignation in her eyes that Sue laughed hysterically. "Come on, dear; we're going home."

At first Milly argued. Hadn't she sent Melvin clear to Junction City to relieve Sue of driving home, using her bad ankle? And now did she intend to leave her, Milly, alone in the big house?

"I've no intention of asking him to drive us home; just let me call for a cab."

91

There was talk of how much a cab would cost, and then Milly threw one arm across her eyes and began to cry. She'd suffered such shock. She'd been through so much. And now when she needed her friend Lovenia with her, Sue was determined to take her away.

She turned to Lovenia, and Lovenia spoke with astonishing firmness. "We're all of us tired out, Milly. We'll feel better for sleeping in our own beds. And it isn't as though Hettie were any kin to you. She was really no more than a servant."

To Milly's, "How can you say that?" she made no answer, but turned to the telephone and herself called for a cab.

Milly turned to Sue then. "Cousin Hettie didn't feel she was," she protested. "I'll show you the note she left. Of course the coroner has it now, but he promised to give it back. Oh, and the one she left you—"

She went to her desk, unlocked a drawer, brought forth the note and handed it to Sue. "You're to say nothing to anyone about this," she ordered.

Sue looked up from the note to Milly. "What difference would it make?"

"I want to keep it. Cousin Hettie was like a mother to me, you know."

Sue made a mental photograph of the short note and handed it to Milly, who in return handed her a heavy man's ring. By then the cab was pulling into the ranch; the headlights were bright before they disappeared behind the first row of hills.

Neither Sue nor her aunt said anything of importance while they were in the cab, and the moment they were in the house Sue hurried to the north door. There was a note there; quickly she read it.

"call the airport, ask for Ben, ask him to bring your car to Lakeville."

Sue placed the call immediately; then, with a sigh of relief at having transportation available in the near future, hurried up to Lovenia's room to find her sitting in a deep chair, her face drained of color.

"Sue," she said, "you must never tell anyone about that note Milly kept."

But why, Aunt Lovey? Not that I would."

"Because *that* is the only note Hettie left. Milly wrote the other. She had to have something to establish Hettie's death as suicide. Everyone would have thought it suspect if the one bit of evidence was left to you, a comparative stranger. So she copied Hettie's handwriting and wrote one to herself."

"How do you know?"

Mrs. Cantrell reached down in her blouse and pulled up a crumpled piece of paper, smoothed it and handed it to Sue.

Here were lines, practice lines of the note Milly was to give the coroner.

"But, Aunt Lovey, if there were an investigation the note could be proved a forgery and then Milly would have placed herself in jeopardy."

"Anyone else, dear, not Milly. Her good works are so public no one, that is no one in political office, would question her. She'll come out of this with her prestige higher than ever. The note she wrote established her as a wonderful woman."

"But it was suicide."

"Unquestionably. I think Hettie had taken all she could take. She was old and penniless. She couldn't get away from Milly any other way. And too," she paused a moment, "she began changing shortly after you came. I think she thought a great deal of you. Perhaps she felt if her death drew a barrier against Milly's activities it would give you time to throw up defenses."

"Then why did Milly show me the true note?"

"Because she had to know how much you knew, how much Hettie had told you. She had to face you with it and judge from your reactions."

"And Melvin questioned me on the way home."

Sue sat in deep thought, then went for her bag and returned with the ring. She studied it a few moments. Just a big signet ring, probably belonging to Hettie's husband at one time. And then Sue tipped it under the reading lamp and saw letters scratched inside.

Slowly she spelled it out. "P-r-a-e-m-o-n-i-t-u-s. It doesn't make sense. Write it down, Aunt Lovey." And she handed her pen and a scrap of paper from her bag.

"Oh," she said sharply when she saw the written word, "it means forewarned. The rest of the quotation is 'forearmed.' This was her real message to me."

She sat a moment frowning, then looked up. "Aunt Lovey, I didn't know anyone could be as unscrupulous as Milly. Why, I doubt she'd stop at murder, if it was to gain an end."

Chapter Ten

It was several days later that Sue again saw Ed Weaver, as she drove past the lumber yard, far to the south of town.

Ed was standing at the gates and motioned her to drive to the right, to where great piles of siding built a temporary wall. Before she drove in Sue saw his car, in which the vivid girl sat patiently waiting.

"Ed," Sue spoke impulsively, "why don't you introduce me to your friend?"

"Friend? Oh, you mean Gypsy. I will in time, Sue. Right now it's better that you know nothing about her. I suppose you agree with the rest of Lakeville that I broke up her home?"

Sue watched the sharply angled shadows of the lumber pile against the yellow ground. "Why, no," she answered. "No outsider breaks up a home. They're just there, outside, waiting to pick up the pieces."

He smiled, then changed the subject. "I want to talk to you about your engagement to Mel. I was given an eyewitness account of it. This person told me you were completely surprised but didn't deny it. Are you in love with Melvin Roth?"

Sue shook her head. "No. I feel terribly sorry for him, but I can't imagine anything worse than marrying a man for whom you feel sorry." She looked up then, her tawny eyes dark with thought. "I believe Milly staged the whole thing. What bothers me is *why*. I'm not what she wants. Darlyn Smyth is crazy about Mel and I think he likes her, and Darlyn is wealthy in her own right, besides being the only heir to her father's money."

"And if Mel married Darlyn the Smyths would have entrée to Milly's personal life," Ed interposed. "You have only your Aunt Lovenia. At that, Sue, I don't think Milly wants you to marry Mel. I think she'd manage to break it up, perhaps at the eleventh moment, but in a way that would discredit you."

"Why?"

"Because she knows she can't manage you as she's managed some. At first you were puzzling. You didn't fight back, so she felt secure. Then she learned you quietly slipped through her fingers."

They were silent, and Sue heard the distant buzz of a saw and the closer buzz of flies and smelled the rich aroma of fresh lumber and felt a nostalgia for her life in Timberton where there were neither Melvins nor Ed Weavers, disrupting the harmony of her life.

"Sue—" she looked up and found Ed looking off toward the far end of the yard, his cheeks quite ruddy— "does Mel—that is—well, does he?"

She could smile a little. "Does he what?"

"Well, does he make any demands, any passes?"

Sue giggled. "Ed, he acts like a maiden aunt. Thank goodness. Mel is a decent sort, you know. He's hardly mentioned the engagement and he hasn't yet produced the ring. So I've let things ride."

Now Ed looked down at her seriously. "Let them, Sue; let them ride as long as you can. There's bound to be a break in this sometime. I know this is true. I also know Milly Mack has something on your aunt that Mrs. Cantrell doesn't realize. Until we can learn what that is, try to play along."

"But I have to find work of some kind whether she approves or not. Ed, is there anything this town doesn't have that I could offer?"

"Yes!" He seemed amazed at realizing it. "There certainly is. Not a library in the place. If you could set up a circulating library, both sides would throng there."

Now Sue was sitting up. "That desolate old

building on the west side of the square. Does Milly own that?"

"No. No, by George, no one in town owns it and I know the man who does. Sue, I think you've got something. I'll ride right over to Junction City and put in a call to him. I think he'd let you have it for a song."

Sue was so excited she almost failed to hear him say something about getting in touch with her the usual way. He'd also check and learn where she could buy up stock for the library.

"Ed," she breathed impulsively, "I don't know what I'd have done without you, what I'd do—"

"I hope you'll never have to learn, Sue."

And then he'd vanished behind the lumber and she was on her way.

Lovenia Cantrell was lying down when Sue came in.

Sue sat near the bed, swinging one slipper vigorously. "Aunt Lovey, why is there no library in Lakeville?"

Lovenia gave her a wry smile. "Because Milly doesn't read, or hadn't you noticed? Actually because this is one of the three counties in the state which hasn't a county library from which Lakeville could draw branch supplies.

"The Lakeville women tried to sponsor a city library but Milly stopped that. But what are you thinking?"

"We, darling, you and I, are going to open a library. And we're going to keep our pretty little mouths shut tight until all of the preliminaries are over, the building checked, the license issued. And then later we'll buy up the license."

"But where, Sue? Milly could order our landlord to break his lease some way."

"Nu-uh. This landlord doesn't live here any more."

When Sue described the building Lovenia sat up. "Of course. It used to be a plumbing shop. Chet Corbin ran it. With no new business coming into Lakeville . . . oh, and, Sue, he hates Milly; isn't that wonderful?"

Sue laughed. She'd never thought the fact someone hated someone else could be called wonderful, but it was.

They couldn't wait to get started until dark, until that late hour when they might expect word from Ed Weaver, so they spent the time cataloguing the books in the Cantrell library.

"Several of my friends gave me gift subscriptions to book clubs," Lovenia told Sue, "so we'll have a good stock of best sellers for the last three years. Then some may want to read the old classics."

Sue had her nose in Trollope's *Orley Farm,* and nodded. "Including your niece. But do you want to risk losing these?"

"Borrowers interested in those will be the type to return them, carefully."

It was fortunate the Cantrell library was so

large, for it would give them work to do in the ensuing days.

That night brought only a note written in a feminine hand. "Gone to investigate bankrupt stock of gift shop and circulating library. Can have first six months lease of shop for payment of taxes and insurance plus one dollar a month."

Milly Mack came to call on the third day but they were prepared for her. They were, they explained when she found them looking dusty and disheveled, cleaning house.

She was full of news. "Sue, someone is going into business in that old building on the west of the square. If you can learn who it is you may be able to find a job, providing of course they need anyone to do clerical work."

"What kind of business?" Sue asked.

"Nobody seems to know. Someone telephoned old man Corbin, but he's so deaf they couldn't make him understand what they wanted to know."

"Mr. Corbin owns the property," Lovenia stated, and Sue remembered to nod.

"The merchants aren't a bit happy about it," Milly went on. "This town has everything it needs, and anyone else thinking they can cut in on legitimate business will find themselves boycotted, except, of course, by the malcontents. But they're too few."

Lovenia started to speak, then closed her lips firmly. As she would tell Sue later, there were a number of stores being run at a profit from the patronage of Milly's malcontents.

"I wouldn't like to work for someone who'd opened a business that couldn't live," Sue said soberly. "It would be like watching something die of malnutrition."

"You're not showing the right spirit, Susan," Milly retorted sharply. "I've told any number of the merchants to speak to the new owner at their first opportunity, to see if they couldn't find work there for you."

Sue closed her eyes. Could it be Milly was finally playing into her hands?

"But would they be able to pay much?" she wondered aloud.

"Better than nothing," Milly flashed with asperity. "And Lovenia knows I'm lenient. I've let her skip any number of payments."

For a moment there was stillness in the room, a stillness that was charged with portent. Sue felt as though she'd received a blow she'd been waiting. She wished she dared signal her aunt, but when she looked at Lovenia, Lovenia was staring at Milly Mack, whose attention was focused on Sue.

"Milly," Lovenia's voice was faint, "I've never missed a payment. Not one."

Milly made one of her quick bird-like movements, going over to Lovenia and laying a hand on her shoulder. "Now, dear, I didn't say that to disturb you but to make you realize you were not in such dreadful straits as you feel. But you *did* skip *quite* a few. Your *mind,* dear, was not at its best at the time. All of your friends noticed how forgetful you were."

Lovenia Cantrell was looking down, and Milly whirled away, laughing a little. "Sue dear, did you know for a while after Mr. Cantrell died—well, really later after she'd been shocked at the dreadful condition of her finances, Lovey couldn't remember the day of the week. As for the months—well—"

"Milly," Sue spoke breathlessly, "how many payments did you say Aunt Lovey missed?"

"What does it matter?" Milly turned back to Lovey. "She's my good friend, isn't she? What more can I do than see her through her troubles?"

Sue was wondering what more she *would* do.

No one spoke for a moment; then Milly said, "Sue, you should go up there right away. There are men cleaning out the inside of the building and painters working outside. Surely they'll know who's coming in."

Sue shook her head. "If they wouldn't tell the Lakeville business men, they'll not tell a comparative stranger. I'll wait." She'd wait until Milly left at last. She'd not leave her aunt alone with her.

"Then I'll drive up and question the men."

Sue walked to the door with her, watched her into her car, and waited until she'd driven away; then she went back to her aunt.

"Lovey, you look like a collapsed balloon."

"But, Sue, don't you realize what she's going to

102

do? Those receipts I couldn't find—somehow she has them or has destroyed them. We don't know how many."

"We know how many you have," Sue reminded her.

"Aunt Lovey, dear, don't worry. Milly wouldn't be throwing her weight around the way she is if she were sure of her power."

Mrs. Cantrell cheered up, especially when Sue pointed out that Milly had practically ordered her to work in the new store.

Milly did more. She stopped on the way back and said she had learned what was going on. "A gift shop and circulating library. A man by the name of Dupre is putting it in and he is interested in a clerk for the shop, one who can 'process' books. So hurry right up there."

"Come on, Aunt Lovey." Sue pulled her aunt to her feet and pushed her toward the stairs. "Go make yourself pretty. You'll excuse us, won't you?"

There was nothing else Milly could do. Sue heard her prowling around downstairs and gave thanks every paper of importance was in a safety deposit box at the county seat bank, and that the library door was locked.

At that she hurried through her dressing and came down to all but usher Milly out and on her way, and to think as she did she would order new locks put on all of the doors.

"I'll call you as soon as I know anything," Sue

promised, and was rewarded by seeing Milly get into her car and head north along the lake boulevard.

Sue sent the little car flying along the shaded streets of Lakeville. "Isn't this a break?" she asked her aunt. "Both of us simply dying to see the place and afraid to go near, and now Milly orders us there."

"Who's this Dupre Milly talked about?"

"We'll soon learn," Sue answered.

It was surprising how much had been accomplished in the short time since Sue had seen the building. The weeds had been cut in the lots on either side, the debris hauled off and the old brick painted a warm cream.

Inside, they could see workmen and one man in business clothes.

Sue went in, and the man turned, and his smile was sudden. "You wouldn't be the Miss Sue Thompson everyone's talking about?" he remarked.

He followed her outside then, and she saw he was laughing inwardly. "I had another Miss Thompson here a little while ago, black-eyed and white-haired, but she'd no sooner called herself Thompson than one of the men said, 'Good afternoon, Mrs. Mack.' "

Sue shuddered a little.

"That's all right. From the description Ed gave me," and now he was laughing aloud, "I couldn't have mistaken you. First time I ever knew old Ed to go completely overboard about a girl."

Sue introduced him to her aunt and the three held a conference, assured no one could overhear.

Mr. Dupre was acting as proxy for Sue. He had leased the building, applied and received a license from the city clerk and had then purchased the bankrupt stock upon which Ed Weaver had passed.

"How much was it?" Sue asked fearfully.

"Only five hundred, value three times as much. And if you don't want to pay it in cash—"

"Oh, but I do."

The gift shop and library would open in Dupre's name with Sue and her aunt hired to operate it. Then Sue would buy it publicly from Dupre. "I'm about to be called back into service," he said. "That will give us the opportunity. And now to plans. What color do you want the interior painted, and the shelves? Go in and look around; I'll follow and ask you what you think about this or that."

Sue knew the colors she wanted, bright, cheerful colors against light-reflecting walls and ceilings. Green, rust, copper, brilliant yellows and splashes of bright blue.

The floors were a problem until Lovenia Cantrell remembered some old rugs she had stored away. "Have the floors scraped and painted."

"But the cost, Aunt Lovey—"

"Mr. Corbin's taking care of that," Dupre said.

105

"When Ed told him, Mrs. Cantrell, that you were to be partner in this business, he remembered something your husband had done for him. There'll be no cost to the work or supplies. And he's sending out an oil heater to keep you comfortable this winter."

Driving home, Sue threatened to tie her aunt down. "You're actually floating," she charged.

"I know, dear, but I'm thinking of so many things we can do. Take our extra big chairs and small tables, put reading lamps beside them. Let our borrowers have time to browse, and what if they do read a book through browsing? And then the Franklyn stove; we'll put that up for the cheer of it."

"Aunt Lovey, if you don't stop you'll be serving meals, and then where would our profit go?"

"We could serve tea. At cost. I'm thinking of the ranch women who come in during the winter. Sometimes they can get through only once a month. How pleasant if they feel free to come in and toast their toes and have a cup of tea while they wait for their husbands."

"But wait. How can we do all of this before we're the acknowledged owners?"

"Sell Mr. Dupre what we expect to want, including my books," answered Lovenia promptly.

They attempted dinner, but Lovenia would arise and wander in to look at some chair or some lamp, return for another bite and be off again. And Sue worried lest she'd arise in the night and go wandering around. She thought of the stairway and by association thought of Milly. Sue hadn't called her.

She went to the telephone immediately.

"My dear, what success did you have?" Milly asked.

"You'd already paved the way," Sue answered. "Both Aunt Lovey and I were hired."

"Lovey! Susan, what are you thinking of! Your aunt is too old."

"Not any more she isn't," Sue caroled. "She's right back to her own age and growing younger. And of course she'll only be there a few hours each day, the rush hours."

"Rush hours?" Milly gave a scoffing little laugh. "Did you want to talk to Melvin?"

"Does he want to talk to me?"

"Sue, you have the strangest way of talking. Of course he does."

"Then he should telephone *me*. Milly."

She turned from the telephone, her eyes bright with annoyance. "It's bad enough being halfway engaged to a man without having our conversations ordered. Oh well, I'd rather it . . . Aunt Lovey, the north door; see if the shades are down in the library."

It was Ed Weaver himself, rather than a note or an emissary. Sue's heart jumped to her throat, performed some strange convolution and returned to thump alarmingly, a sensation half of delight, half of apprehension.

"Something's happened," she said, "something new?"

"Can we go where there is no chance of anyone outside seeing or listening in? And where I can slip out if necessary?"

"But it won't be necessary," Sue assured him. "I've just talked to Milly and she offered to call Melvin."

"You should have taken her up. His car is parked up the boulevard and he's sitting across the street on one of the benches, watching the house."

Sue sighed. "I just can't think fast enough to keep up with her."

Ed Weaver smiled down at her. "It takes more than one. Together we're not doing too badly. And I think I have some good news this time."

They went into the library while Mrs. Cantrell went upstairs, after turning off living room lights, to turn on a low light in Sue's room and one in her own.

Sue waited expectantly while Ed patted the pockets of his sports jacket, then brought out an envelope.

"I received this when I returned to town today, a registered letter mailed two days after Cousin Hettie's death. It was sent from the city."

Wonderingly Sue took out the papers inside the long envelope, a note and a second envelope. She read the note first.

Dear Mr. Weaver, whoever-you-are, the wife and I were vacationing on the lake, returning a few days ago. En route we passed the entrance to an estate and found an old lady standing there. She was quite upset because the mail carrier had passed before she'd reached the highway.

She seemed so distressed we stopped, and she asked if we'd mail the enclosed to you by registered mail so it would reach you on your birthday. She suggested one or two towns near the city where this might be done.

Frankly, we forgot about it until we reached home, so if your birthday passed without a remembrance from an old friend, please blame it on us and also accept our wishes for many happy returns.

Sincerely,

J.C. Mason

Sue looked up at Ed, who nodded toward the envelope. She looked first at the outside, the painfully pencilled scrawl of an arthritic hand; then quickly she opened it.

Another note and a sheaf of slips with a rubber band around them.

The second note read:

Dear Mr. Weaver, I know from what I've heard to be contrary that you can be trusted to carry out my last wish. I have taken the only means I have to get the enclosed to the rightful owner. I am trusting to Divine Providence to send someone along the highway to whom I can entrust this.

I will be dead by the time you receive these. If you wish to right a great wrong please take this to the niece of Lovenia Cantrell, but only when you are sure you will not be seen.

Sue stopped there, slipped the band from the sheaf and found, as she by this time expected, the missing receipts for payments her aunt had made to Milly Mack.

And then she read on:

Tell her she is dealing with a completely unscrupulous woman and needs to be on guard every moment.

I should wait and help to see her through, but the pain is too great and the doctor is not called.

The signature was a weak scrawl, and then there was a postscript.

There is one more paper Mrs. Cantrell should have. I don't know what it is. She

*keeps it in the safe. She took the receipts out
when she intended to foreclose (just before
little Sue came to Lakeville) and left them in
her desk.*

"One more paper," said Sue, and then her eyes
filled with tears. "That line, Ed, 'The pain is too
great and the doctor isn't called.' Can't we do
something about a woman like Milly?"

Chapter Eleven

Watching Ed Weaver, Sue thought he was
weighing his answer to her. She believed he was
careful because he felt knowing too much would
place her in greater danger. Yet she wanted to
know everything.

"Sue, Milly Mack has reached her place of
power by staying carefully within the law. Hettie
didn't say Milly had stolen these receipts. Milly
could prove, by her friends, that your aunt's mind
was vague, and that she was keeping them for
her."

"But can we just sit back and let her go on and
on?"

He smiled at her, and for a moment she forgot

the tragedy of Hettie. "We're not, Sue. And don't worry about your aunt too much."

"Don't worry?" Sue spoke passionately. "How can I help it after what's happened? I wish now I'd just bundled Aunt Lovey into my car and run off with her. Fighting Milly isn't worth the victory."

"That's it, Sue. That's what too many thought, and each time she won she won assurance, money and power. You might say that's what's wrong with the world today, the reluctance of right-thinking people to fight for the small principle because to them it isn't worth the battle."

He was ready to leave and she didn't want him to go. She wanted him to stay right where he was so she could watch the glint of the low light on his hair, the shadows forming under his firm chin. And as long as he was here he wasn't with Gypsy. She tried to think of fresh questions, fresh problems to detain him.

"Ed, why is Mel watching the house?"

Now that she spoke of it she was half frightened.

He looked at her, suddenly alert. "You say Milly asked if you wanted to speak to him. Sue, something tells me that was a leading question. She doesn't know where he is. And that makes me feel better about his being around here."

A car rushing by gave two swift honks and Ed stood up. "That's my signal Mel's on his way home."

Sue walked to the north door and stood, still reluctant to see him leave. With his going went her feeling of all being right in her world. "Ed, how can I thank you for checking the stock, finding the building owner and Dupre, everything?"

Even in the dark she could see the gleam of white teeth as he laughed. "Well, I would like to see your aunt settled into a pleasant, easy job that would assure her a living. There's my car again."

Sue stalked through the hall, indignant. Not that she didn't love her aunt. But here she'd been silly enough to think that Ed Weaver was doing these things for her.

She was halfway upstairs when the telephone rang. She went on slowly, made her way to the bed lamp her aunt had turned off after a proper period, and turned it on. Within a minute the telephone stopped.

Sue left the light on as one would if waiting for further bells, then flipped it off and went to her aunt's room. "Milly checking on Mel," she said wearily. "Aunt Lovey, that timing was perfect. Is there anyone else at the Macks' besides Mel and Milly?"

"They have a man who takes care of the stock and does the gardening. He never appears when anyone's there. His face has been badly burned. Why?"

"Oh, I was just wondering how Milly could look through the telescope and be telephoning at the same time. I'd replace those light shades with blackout blinds if it wouldn't be telling her what I knew."

And then she brightened. "Goodness, I almost forgot the good news. Before Cousin Hettie died she mailed the missing receipts to Ed Weaver."

"To Ed Weaver!" cried Lovenia. "Why that particular person?"

"Because Cousin Hettie wasn't stupid. Ed brought them tonight, but I had him take them away again until I can get in to the county seat and put them in our safety deposit box. Well, to sleep."

"My dear, and how I shall sleep after that blessed news?"

There was no question about the success of the Lakeville Library. It held two formal openings. At the first there were so many flowers a tourist asked if a wedding was in progress.

Milly Mack presided at the tea table, and the elite of Lakeville thronged in. All made the necessary deposit for membership, a few rented books, but most purchased bits of pottery for future bridge parties.

The second opening was held that evening. Sue, returning from a quickly snatched sandwich at the corner drugstore, looked upon the place and found it delightful. People thronged the book section. An individual walking aimlessly, nose in a book, finally stumbled on a chair, to sink into it and, by the light of stand lamps, go on reading. A few groups here and there held animated discussions, books in hand rather the worse for wear as points were pounded out.

None of this group purchased gifts, but all went out balancing stacks of books.

The girl Gypsy came in a jeep with several young veterans' wives, from the other side of the lake. When she came up to Sue's desk and found they were alone for the moment, she smiled and said, "Some day soon, we're going to be friends."

Sue glanced up after she had made out a card to Gypsy Ladue and wondered suddenly if the vivid clothes she wore were a camouflage. The blue eyes seemed filled with pain and were dark with shadows.

"Need we wait?" she asked.

"A little while." And she moved on.

Just before they closed Ed Weaver came in, found the non-fiction shelf and came up to the desk. "This is better than the north door in an emergency," he said softly; and without smiling, "Incidentally, the usual audience is parked across the street, so you don't know me."

Sue caught the warning and checked him out without more than a bare lift of the head and a formal smile.

On Saturday the ranch women came in, swooped in, it seemed to Sue and her aunt. When they heard they might return books by mail they grew rapturous.

"Now I can face another winter," declaimed one. "The mail can get through when we can't get the car to the highway; for this I'll slide to the post box and climb back."

Milly Mack thought they were foolish to offer such service. "You're going to get in trouble with your boss," she prophesied. "You'll mail books out to these women and never hear of them again and be out postage."

"But they're leaving a ten dollar deposit." Sue said gently. "Ten dollars will pay for quite a number of books and postage."

Milly Mack was in and out until Sue and Lovenia wondered who was running the place.

"I don't like it," Lovenia said. "Milly never shows this much enthusiasm unless she's to benefit."

Sue said nothing. The business men were beginning to stream in, their lunch hours cut short that they might browse without running into the afternoon group.

" 'Tell me what a man reads and I'll tell you'—" Sue didn't finish the quotation but shook her head. "Imagine Mr. Foss wanting nothing but high adventure. But then banking is a bit routine."

"And James Clive, the high school principal, devours mysteries," contributed Lovenia. "What is Martin, the barber, reading?"

"Nuclear physics," groaned Sue. "What a blessing Uncle Ned had such catholic taste. We can supply almost anything."

Yes, their venture was going to succeed. By the third week they were sure of it. The newness had worn off, but still people came and seemed coming more often and staying longer.

"I swear," Lovenia yawned one night, "I'm going to bring an alarm clock so they'll know it's time for us to close."

They were drawing a curious group in the evening. Men en route to club or lodge would drop their wives at the library. Wives, intent upon some club or auxiliary meeting, would be driven to their destination; then the husbands would return to the library.

Ed Weaver, coming in one night, remarked, "You'd better rename this. It's not a library; it's a community club."

Sue nodded and sighed. "Then I wish we could elect a chairman and have proceedings conducted by Roberts' Rules of Order. We've had some fearful rows."

"How do you handle them?" Ed asked curiously.

"The last time I picked up my big *Silence* sign and paraded up and down. It worked. For that time."

"What does your sponsor think about it?"

Sue looked up, puzzled. "My sponsor?"

"Didn't you know Milly is letting it be known that she's behind this? Her way of dispensing charity to your aunt, and incidentally you?"

Sue sat very still. Could it be that Ed Weaver was trying to psychologize her into futher antagonism toward Milly?

"Why are you telling me this?" she asked.

"Because Milly is trying to make her story true. She's approached Dupre twice to try to buy this out. The second time she started an investigation and learned he hadn't the money to handle it in the first place."

"We should have been open about it in the beginning."

"Don't blame yourself; but be on guard. Right?"

"Thank you, Ed." And she watched him stride quickly out to the car where Gypsy waited and wondered why she must always associate his presence with some new and disturbing problems.

Milly struck the next day. She came in as they opened up, and there was no pretense of friendliness on her face when she made her demand.

"I want this shop. Tell me how much you've invested and I'll add five per cent."

Sue met her glance and refused to look away. "It isn't for sale, Milly. It provides us with the income we need."

"Why did you lie to me about Dupre?"

"I didn't. You assumed certain conditions and I didn't correct you."

Milly considered this a moment, then laughed. "Well, congratulations. You'll be wanting to sell before the winter's over. Let me know when you're ready."

And then she turned on Lovenia. "You needn't have sent your payment if your funds were so low

118

Sue had to take care of it for you. I was utterly shocked to receive that cashier's check from Timberton."

"Isn't it right I should pay rent for a home?" Sue asked, before Lovenia could speak. "And it has nothing to do with her funds."

"But why the cashier's check? Sue, did you think I wouldn't honor a personal check from you?"

Sue smiled. "Perhaps I'm a bit remiss about remembering dates. I knew the bank wouldn't be."

Milly stood for another moment, then tipped her head to one side, "I didn't know you were so affluent. Girls in clerical positions don't receive very high wages, or do they?"

"I received enough to live comfortably without drawing on my inheritance."

Milly nodded, tapped a long hand on her bag, then laughed. "Melvin was wiser than I thought. Well, I have a great deal of business this morning."

She left. Sue and Lovenia remained frozen to the spots where they'd been standing; then Lovenia collapsed into a deep chair. "Sue, you should feel ready to be hung out. If anyone was ever put through a wringer. At that, she took the news much better than I'd dared hope."

"I wonder!" muttered Sue, then swung angrily. "I'm so tired of having to pull my punches. But I have the feeling if I ever let her anger me to the point of slapping facts at her, she'll win."

"Sue," her aunt mused one morning at breakfast, "I'd like to put in a knitting section. Lakeville women are having to send outside for their wool, and all of these young women coming in are either learning to knit or want to."

"Would you act as instructor?"

"I don't know enough. But little old Mrs. Kane would jump at the chance. She lives with her daughter and they're having a struggle to make ends meet. She could charge for lessons and we'd take our profit on wool sales and other supplies."

Sue looked at her aunt, blinked and looked again. Could this brisk, competent-looking woman be the cowed old lady she'd found when she reached Lakeville?

"I think it's a wonderful idea," Sue said.

And so a new clientele was added; women not interested in reading or buying pottery came to buy wool or sit in the far corner of the building where a delighted Agnes Kane held fort.

It was late on Saturday afternoon of the Labor Day week-end. In a lull Sue sat, conscious of wilting under the steady heat. Mel was taking her to dinner some place in the country, Mel and one of the young married couples Milly approved.

Milly's friend Nora Carmandy stepped up. "This place," Mrs. Carmandy informed Sue, "is getting to be a veritable hotbed of scandal. Look at those two back there."

Sue looked back and surpressed a smile. Two men, facing each other so close there was scarcely

120

an inch between their respective noses, were arguing angrily. She looked further and saw two more trying to avoid each other, and still further a group of women whispering with the hissing of alarmed geese.

"It's the only place in Lakeville such conditions could exist!" declared Mrs. Carmandy.

Sue felt the flick of awareness. Of course. It was the only place in Lakeville where people on opposite sides of the political fence could meet.

"Well?" demanded Milly's friend. "Do you intend to do anything about it? I'd suggest you ask that element to stay away."

Sue glanced down at the books she was processing. "Good for all of them," she said lightly. "It will lower the mortality rate. Just think of the repressions they're releasing. Besides," and now she looked directly at the woman, "all intelligent people like to hear both sides of a question. Lakeville people are intelligent, aren't they?"

"*Well!*" gasped Mrs. Carmandy, grabbed her books and vanished.

Sue signaled her aunt and Lovenia came over to relieve her. "I only want to stretch," Sue said, "and listen in," she added.

"Take your time and don't bother with that stack of books on the rear table. Someone brought them in as a contribution to our stock. I'll mark them and put them up later."

Sue wandered back to the shelf the other side of which the two men were engaged in their verbal duel. Of course, it was the school election over which they were fighting. The newer citizens had gained enough signatures on their petition to have the school bond issue placed on the ballot in the coming election. Now they were doing everything to foster its passage, and were meeting bitter opposition.

"I grew up in Lakeville," Pendleton Sharp was bleating. "I was educated in the Lakeville schools. I was accepted at the University without any question."

"Yeah?" interrupted Martin West. "And how many eons ago was that? Things have changed since you attended Lakeville schools. Universities are a darned sight more particular who they let in. They haven't the time to—"

"Why, you, you nincompoop. I'll bet you weren't able to finish grammar—"

"They call it grade school now, Mister Sharp."

Sue rounded the end of the shelves, and the two men wheeled on her.

To Mr. Smart, Miss Thompson was the niece of an old time citizen of Lakeville, solid, conservative. Also, wasn't she engaged to Melvin Roth?

To Mr. West, Miss Thompson was young and intelligent enough to weigh issues and reach the right answer.

"And how do *you* feel about this school bond issue?" they asked in unison.

Sue answered easily, "As you know, I haven't

lived here long enough to register. As I'm not eligible to vote, I haven't considered it."

They rained convictions on her. Surely she'd heard it discussed, as she was making Lakeville her home, she must take an interest in everything affecting it. It was impossible for her not to have formed some opinion.

Sue shook her head. "As I haven't property to be taxed if the issue wins, or children to be deprived of certain benefits if it doesn't, I haven't felt I had the right to an opinion."

And when they shot further questions at her she laughed. "All right, I do have one opinion: that Lakeville is not voting on the school board members or the bond issue." And leaving them to figure that out, she returned to her desk.

Lovenia arose, memo pads and card pockets in one hand, paste pot in the other. "I'll take care of those books now so they'll be available to late-comers," she said.

Two subdued opponents walked up to the desk to present their books and eye Sue suspiciously. Each wanted to ask what she'd meant and neither wanted to let the other realize he didn't know.

Sue was working on the first pile when a scream came from the group of women. She looked back and saw them rushing across the rear of the room; then one called, "Miss Thompson, call a doctor."

There were cries of "Water" and "She's fainted" and "Look, she's coming to."

Sue had reached the knot of women by then

and wondered hysterically why people could pass the most rigorous first aid examination, then crowd around a fainting person.

Martin West reached Lovenia Cantrell before Sue. "Get back, you cackling hens," he yelled. "Hey, Sharp, open that window."

The doctor who had come to Sue's call another time pushed through and knelt beside Lovenia. He looked at her, then at something lying beside her, and quickly opened his bag and prepared a hypodermic.

"What's the matter, Doctor?" a chorus asked.

"Heat," he answered; "fainted. Mr. Sharp, will you ask everyone to leave? West, isn't there one of those chairs with a lounge back? Good. Miss Thompson, can you heat a cup of something, coffee if you have it here?"

Sharp and West returned and the doctor turned to Mr. Sharp quickly.

"Do you have your car handy? If you could take Mrs. Cantrell—"

"Of course, of course." And Sharp was off.

It was then the doctor looked up. "Shock," he said, and Sue went back to the water she'd left heating.

West and the doctor lifted Lovenia to the lounge chair where she lay shaking with a chill. They borrowed a wool afghan from the wool display and tucked that over her; then Sue came with the coffee which had to be fed to her spoon by spoon until she could grasp the cup.

"So silly," she said, and began to laugh. "When I was seven, at school, boy threw a snake around my neck." She began shaking again. "It crawled inside. He told me it was a rattler."

"But—" Sue began, and then the doctor nodded to the book which lay where Lovenia had dropped it when she fell.

Sue went over to it and saw the book had come apart, evidently at Lovenia's touch. Both parts showed vivid colored plates of rattlesnakes, coiled to strike.

The doctor looked at Sue. "Would you like to call Doctor Devaux?"

"No!" said Lovenia sharply, and Sue echoed it.

"Then I'll call this evening. You'll be all right now. Incidentally, I'll take that book with me; then I want you to repair it and put it back on the shelf. And, West, Miss Thompson and Mrs. Cantrell, tell no one about this. You merely fainted from the heat."

The men carried Lovenia to Mr. Sharp's car at the rear of the building, but Sue went to the front to follow in her coupe. There were still knots of people waiting, asking if there was any way they could rent books for the long week-end.

"Miss Thompson," Gypsy Ladue stepped up, "I used to be a librarian. Could I help you?"

"You wouldn't mind?" Sue asked anxiously.

Gypsy laughed. "Knowing what to expect, not at all."

One or two of the women turned away, but

curiosity got the better of them, and when Sue finally went to her car she found the place thronged, Gypsy in her usual colorful clothes entrenched at the desk.

At home, with Lovenia lying down, Doctor Fuller said, "I'll have to talk fast because I've an idea Mrs. Mack will be down here before long. Now, Mrs. Cantrell, do many people know of your phobia?"

Lovenia laughed guiltily. "Practically everyone. I have a genius for finding any snake on any picnic."

'I'm sure you realize that book was planted there for your to pick up. Do you know why?"

"Heckling, I suppose. Someone wants to buy us out."

Sue looked at the doctor. He seemed satisfied.

He said he'd be over the next morning. "And then we'll go after this. The best way to cure a phobia is to face it, not run away from it. When you run away your imagination takes over. We'll go through that book and look at snakes, learn their habits. They are really quite interesting. Now don't look like that." He laughed.

Sue went with him to the door where he stood with a withdrawn look in his eyes; then he moved. "Later, I'll take her a step further," he told Sue. "I want her to be able to suggest that book to a patron, open it, show the plates."

Sue looked her question, but he said nothing more.

Well, at least she had an excuse to break her dinner date, and to spend a delightfully lazy weekend. Only one thing bothered her. She must drive south to the nearest city for the purchase of additional books; it would be a two day trip. She'd let it go for another week.

Milly Mack drove in a few moments after Sue had telephoned her regrets to Melvin. Milly was in a righteously indignant mood. Didn't this prove the work was too hard for "Lovey"? "Also, I was told that you put that woman in as librarian."

"And happy to have someone experienced," agreed Sue.

"But do you know her?"

"Only from seeing her around town and in the library. From her choice of books, I'd consider her unusually intelligent."

"Do you call it intelligent to get mixed up with a man like Ed Weaver? To live alone in the same house with him and pose as brother and sister when it's proven they're not? Why, when I heard that I had my—that is, I had them investigated. I learned her maiden name was Demarset and proved his was Weaver. He was born in Chicago and she in New Orleans and they didn't meet until after she was married."

Sue felt a sickness inside; then she thought of Ed Weaver and of Gypsy's clear eyes and asked curiously, "Why were they of enough importance to you to investigate?"

"Aren't you being impertinent, Susan?" flashed Milly.

Sue shrugged her shoulders. "You brought up the subject."

Milly stood ready to leave. "Someone has to look after the interests of Lakeville. We've made it a clean, decent little town. And, Susan, we intend to keep it that way."

Sue closed the door behind Milly Mack softly and returned to her aunt. Lovenia was sitting up, looking perturbed. "Sue," she said, "that sounded to me like a declaration of war."

"You're about three months behind time, Aunt Lovey. Or no, you're right. Heretofore it's been police action. Now it's open warfare. All right, let it be. If she'll fight in the open—"

"You know she won't, Sue."

Sue nodded and stood a moment in angry thought. "Clean, decent. Imagine calling Lakeville that. Why, Lakeville has the vilest accumulation of tongues I've ever heard hiss. If anyone ever said anything loving about anyone else I'd fall flat in a dead faint."

"Sue," Lovenia was disturbed, "use your imagination. What could Milly do to defeat us?"

Sue saw again the postscript on Cousin Hettie's letter, but answered quickly, "By squeezing us out of business, by sending out an order not to patronize us."

When she thought of what that could mean Sue felt chilled. She had used most of her inheritance to pay off the claim against the Cantrell home and for the shop and library stock. If Milly were to order those under her control to stop patronizing the place, they could be forced to close up.

They didn't see handwriting on the wall, next morning; they did see bold black print on the editorial page of the town's one newspaper. It read:

PLAN TO CORRUPT LAKEVILLE
WITH SALACIOUS LITERATURE.

Chapter Twelve

Susan saw the editorial first. She was curled up in a basket chair in the summerhouse enjoying a leisurely third cup of coffee and wondering how she could manage a release from the evening's dinner at Milly's.

Lovenia, moving about her garden, was too visibly recovered to offer as an excuse. Lovenia, she noticed, was supremely happy. She was snipping off dead zinnia heads and long-stemmed asters for the table with equal fervor, pausing now and then to look out on the lake and the far mountains.

And then Susan, turning a page, saw the caption and felt her heart stand still. She glanced at her aunt, still absorbed in the garden, and began to read. Once she stiffened indignantly, but soon a smile touched her lips and once her shoulders shook convulsively. Finally she gave up and laughed aloud.

"Sue, what on earth?" asked Lovenia.

"The first shot in the battle, but I'm sure it's going to boomerang. I wander who wrote it. I'll bet the editor is grinding his teeth."

Lovenia handed the asters to Sue to put in water while she read, and when Sue returned her aunt had a peculiar expression on her face, half amused, half frightened.

"I have a feeling Milly wrote this," Lovenia said. "You know she fancies herself as a writer."

"But she never reads," protested Sue.

Lovenia laughed. "That's how she maintains her illusion. And of course she owns the controlling interest in this newspaper. That's the first thing she purchased when she arrived here."

"Arrived?" Sue looked her interest. "I'd assumed she'd been here forever."

"No, only about ten years. However, back to this editorial. A lot of people are going to agree with her."

"Not the intelligent ones and not the readers. Aunt Lovenia, I'd be willing to bet she can't coerce the book addicts. I know them. They'll buy bootleg service if they're not free to come in openly."

Lovenia shrugged her shoulders. "That remains to be seen. Meanwhile we'd better prepare for company. Everybody and his pet pup are going to call today to watch our reaction."

Doctor Foster was the first to call. He arrived with a wicked grin in his eyes. "Congratulations," he said. "What a nice piece of free advertising the morning paper gave you."

"You really think so?" asked Lovenia.

"As a friend of mine, said this morning, it's as good as having a book suppressed in Boston. You'll have patrons who never read a book before."

The doctor and Sue's aunt settled comfortably in the summerhouse, the big book on reptiles in the doctor's lap. Sue listened for a little while as he led up to the subject of rattlesnakes by discussing the non-poisonous ones.

"I'd never thought of them as being of any use," she said once, when he described them as scavengers and the police of the rodent world.

And Lovenia said half-heartedly, "If I could rent the service of a King snake to clear my garden of gophers, I do believe I could tolerate him."

He was telling of coming upon a mother snake guarding her young and how snakes struck only in fear, when Sue heard the telephone.

It was Milly at her most cordial. Would little Sue mind if their week-end engagements were cancelled altogether? Her guests were going out to a ranch, a house party and as Sue should remain with her aunt, after her dreadful shock, Darly Smith would take her place.

Sue wondered if she dared show the relief she felt, but said of course she wouldn't mind, she had so much to do at home. Leaving the telephone, she wondered what interpretation Milly would put upon the cancelled engagement.

She heard all about it during the day.

"I see you're not wearing your engagement ring," offered one.

Sue smiled. "Never having had an engagement ring, I couldn't wear one."

"Oh? I understood you and Melvin had quarrelled over the type of books you carry in that library of yours."

And now Sue laughed. "No, I've never been with Mel long enough to work up to a quarrel. More tea?"

Much to the amazement of Lovenia, who knew how Lakeville husbands guarded the sacred privacy of Sunday afternoons, a number of women were accompanied by their husbands who showed by looks if not by words that they sympathized with Sue and Lovenia.

The last visitor brought a note, and Sue, taking it from the hands of Mr. Foss, was amazed. Surely this bank manager wasn't ready to risk losing the biggest depositor and stockholder in his bank. But the note was from Ed Weaver.

How about meeting the other half? If you'd like a barbecue with us will pick you up north end of garden shortly after eight-thirty.

Sue would put that evening down in her memory as a dream of pure delight, the more vivid for the nightmares she had been enduring.

It was one of the young wives who came for them. "Protection from gossip," she announced gaily.

They drove west toward Junction City, turning south on a narrow road which wound then around the southern end of the lake, then north through the settlement of modest new homes and thence to a beach where a great fire showed a mass of figures moving back and forth.

Ed Weaver met them as they drove up, and now Sue knew it was a dream, for he had time for no one else. And Gypsy didn't seem to mind. Gypsy, Sue remembered, was from New Orleans, and it was she who made the salad and the barbecue sauce and who picked out the choice bits of everything for Sue and her aunt.

Good food and then good talk, spirited and impersonal. Not that voices didn't raise, but there was no rancor in them. It was possible, Sue saw, to differ violently, yet concede one's opponent a right to his perspective.

And always there was Ed Weaver putting in the right word at the right time.

"Want to visit my cabin before you leave?" he asked. "Remember, Sue, the logs were delivered that day we met?"

And Sue remembered a voice shouting down about the delivery of logs.

He drove them to a bank above the lake where a log cabin stood surrounded by oaks.

"Built it myself with help from everybody and his second cousin. What do you think of it?"

It was attractive but like a barracks. Sue looked at the long narrow living room and knew no feminine hand had touched it. There were two bedrooms in a loft reached by an open stairway with a gallery overlooking the living room. Here too was the evidence of male occupancy.

"Now the kitchen," Ed let them back down to the long narrow room flanking the living room, "would have been two by four if Gypsy hadn't arrived in time. She made me copy a plan of her former home. Plenty of working surface, lots of shelves, and instead of another bunk room at the end, that glassed in dinette."

Gypsy. Sue felt a chill clear down to her heels. Gypsy had designed this heavenly kitchen for her own use, of course. Yet would Gypsy, with her love of color, have allowed these windows, like all the other windows, to remain bare?

"Gypsy says she'll make drapes and things when I can decide what kind and color I want. What would be your choice, Sue?"

"Mine?" Sue came back with a start. "But that depends upon the persons living here."

"Pretend this is your house."

It wasn't fair, but Sue thrust down that thought and in a moment was rambling through the house, eyes bright.

"Take your time and write it down," he suggested. "After what you've done to the plumbing shop I feel safe in your hands."

He then showed them the log compound, an enclosed paved area with garage, work shop and supply house. "For we do get snowed in occasionally, I hear."

And Lovenia Cantrell laughed softly. "You beach-comber," she said.

One of the couples drove them home and insisted upon coming in and checking through the house. "To be sure no prowlers came in your absence," the man explained, and though they laughed they were glad to have him.

And Sue went to bed more mystified than ever. Ed and Gypsy. But they weren't living in the same house, as Milly had said. From the young wife who had picked them up, Sue had gleaned Ed was there for meals only. Also that he had purchased the house for Gypsy, using his G.I. loan privileges.

The next day was one of rest. The only one Sue had, for Tuesday brought a steady stream of borrowers to the library. Defiant women came in to purchase from the gift stock, high school and pre-college girls to take last minute lessons in sweater knitting and to purchase wool.

Wednesday Sue looked at the bookshelves and said, "Looks as though a dentist had gone wild with extractions. Aunt Lovey, I must get into the city and bring up a fresh stock. I can't wait for a delivery. But I hate leaving you alone."

Agnes Kane looked up from turning the heel of a sock. "Lovey, why not stay with daughter and me? We'd love having you."

At that Sue dreaded leaving her aunt. While she waited for her car to be serviced she walked toward the bank. Old Mr. Kirby was stumbling along, something unusual, as he ordinarily walked briskly, his head high.

When he responded to Sue's greeting she saw his faded blue eyes were tear-washed and somehow felt he had been hurt. "I need a cup of coffee." she told him, "and I don't like to go into the cafe alone. You wouldn't squire, me, would you?"

"Why, Miss Thompson, I'd be delighted."

His shoulders came up and his head was high as he escorted Sue down the main street, one old hand under her elbow as though she were the most fragile of beings.

His story came out over coffee. He'd been in love with Betty Lou Kelly for the last ten years. Betty Lou was a widow woman and liked him, but Lakeville people made so much fun of them Betty Lou's children told her she must not see him again.

"A man living alone can't do for himself properly," he confided, "so I wrote one of these matrimonial bureaus. I corresponded with a woman who seemed just what I needed. I was honest. I told her I lived on the old age pension with a bit of day work here and there to help out, but that I owned my home and it was comfortable, winter

136

and summer. Then finally, after we'd exchanged photos and all, I sent her money to come here. I went to Junction City to meet her and she didn't get off the bus. This morning I received this."

Dear Bill, because I still think of you that way. Two Lakeville women were on the bus and when I told them I was going there to meet you they made so much ridicule I figured I just couldn't stand living in a town like that.

I'm ashamed now I didn't get off the bus and tell you but I didn't have the courage.

If you ever move to a place where people don't make fun of old folks who are looking for companions, let me know. Lakeville isn't for me. Those two wasted seventy-five miles of scenery talking nasty about their neighbors.

Mrs. Dolly Day.

Sue read the letter and said, "Oh, well, she couldn't have had much courage; you're really better off—"

He cocked his head at her. "Miss Thompson, have you ever been tittered at?"

Impulsively Sue spoke. "Which do you like the better, Betty Lou or Dolly?"

"Dolly, because she hasn't children to boss her around."

"Then give me her address. I'm going down to the city now. I'll call on her and show her there are a few decent people left in Lakeville. Aunt Lovenia will make her happy if she'll come back with me."

Sue drove out of Lakeville, taking her indignation out on the car. She zipped up hills and rounded curves with a screeching of tires.

She reached the city in the late afternoon and after dinner set forth to locate Dolly Day. She found her in an unsavory part of the city, in a one-room housekeeping unit grey with age, and Dolly Day seemed as defeated as her background.

When she heard Sue had come as an emissary from William Kirby she all but wept. "Don't let him know where you found me. This was all I could afford. You see I'd spent so much buying new house-dresses and pretty things for a trousseau. Then, too, I had to pay my fare home and pay to have my trunk and boxes freighted back."

Sue sat burning with anger. The careless, vicious talk of two women had cost this lonely old woman more than money and heartache; it had cost her a faith in future happiness.

"But those two women aren't the only women in Lakeville. My aunt is a wonderful person."

"It wasn't that so much as the way they ridiculed a mail-order marriage, not that that was what this was. We'd met and exchanged references. We couldn't do more because the bus

138

fare was costly. If you could have heard the snide remarks—"

Sue rode out of town the second morning after, a perky Dolly Day sitting beside her, the back of the car filled with Dolly's lares and penates; a beloved antique table she hadn't been able to ship, bound with quilts and tied on behind with ropes.

They passed through Junction City an hour before sunset and were well up the hill when Sue saw a peculiar figure trudging up the hill ahead. As she made curve after curve she saw the figure deposit a heavy old-fashioned suitcase, rest a minute, change it to another hand and trudge on a few steps further.

They came alongside of him on a fairly level curve, and Sue braked to look at the man. He was old, his clothes green with equal age, but his face as pink and white as that of a baby.

"If you don't mind a little crowding we'd be happy to have you ride with us," Sue offered.

The old gentleman stepped up, removed his hat and scrutinized Sue with keen black eyes. "I'd appreciate a ride," he said. "I find I missed the last bus to Lakeville. Is it far?"

"My goodness yes," Sue breathed, then introduced Mrs. Day and said, "I'm Sue Thompson."

"Yes," the little man's big head nodded, "yes," as though affirming something, "and my name is Isidore Duncan."

They tucked him in and started on their way, Mrs. Day chatting happily. This, she informed him, was her first trip to Lakeville, She was going to be married. Did he, she asked anxiously, think her an old fool?

He turned then and looked at her, shaking his head. "Did you ever find a rose in your garden after every other bloom had died? It didn't have the lush beauty of the spring rose, but it held a beauty and fragrance of its own. The companionship of the aged is a November rose."

Sue sent the car ahead with a feeling of exhilaration. What a wonderful old man. But what would Lakeville do to him? A poor old chap in what must surely be second hand clothes. Well, she'd see he wasn't hurt too much.

They topped the ridge and Sue parked a moment to let them look down on Lakeville, their future home. The sun, in moving south, had reached a notch in the ridge and now poured through, washing the town in gold, touching the yellow of turning leaves, sending a path of living light across the lake.

"How peaceful," said Mr. Duncan.

"Peaceful!" Sue and Dolly Day cried their derision in unison.

"What causes the disharmony?" asked the old man.

Sue answered eagerly, "I think it's the influence of one woman. She's like a rotten apple in a bin. Those nearest are touched with her rot, and when these in turn touch the next—"

"But, my dear child," protested Isidore Duncan, "human beings are not apples. An apple has no intelligence, no sense to detect the proximity of rot, nor has it the necessary legs to remove itself to a healthier location. And what is wrong with the people of Lakeville that they haven't the courage to remove the spoiled one from their midst?"

Sue thought of her own relationship with Milly Mack. For the first time in her life she had believed it necessary to lie, to evade, in short, to turn herself into a totally different character from what she'd been before coming to Lakeville.

"It's fear," she said slowly, "fear of reprisal. It's easy to be brave when you've only yourself to consider, but when there is someone else dependent upon you—"

Mr. Duncan leaned forward so he could look directly at Sue. "What is the worst that could have happened to your dependent and you faced the issue?"

"Why, she could have—" Sue stopped and reviewed the farce of the last months—"lost her home," she concluded lamely.

"And perhaps her life," came in a whisper from Isidore Duncan.

Chapter Thirteen

With one movement Sue had the ignition on, the car in gear, and had started downhill, the nameless fear of weeks identified.

"Miss Thompson," Mr. Duncan's voice was strong," need you drive so fast? And you didn't answer my question."

"Question?" Sue slowed the car. "I thought you made a statement."

"You did, Mr. Duncan," said Dolly Day.

"If I did," he stopped, "it was because my old mind reverts to another country at times, another country where a woman lost her life because she defied authority. But that was a country where there was no redress. How nice the lights look down there."

Sue looked down and at that precise moment could see the library windows. They were squares of yellow. She relaxed and laughed at herself. Yet there remained the faintest twinge of apprehension, as though she had inadvertently received a warning.

"If you'll tell me where you're going I can drive you directly there," Sue offered.

Mr. Duncan chuckled. "Well, now if you can

tell me where an old man like myself can find a room to rent, that's where I'll go."

Sue thought of the only hotel and the exorbitant fees they asked. She knew there were no other rooms except at the still full motels. She couldn't just dump him off on the main street.

"There isn't any place but the hotel," she said doubtfully.

And then she heard herself saying, "Why don't you come to my aunt's? Now don't protest; we'd like to have you. It will be a relief to have a man in the house."

"If you can call such an ancient mariner protection," he countered. "Do you have any kin the town doesn't know about? Some distant great-uncle on your mother's—"

Sue laughed happily. "My father's side. No one knows anything about him. Hello, Uncle Izzy."

"Hello, little Sue." Then he looked at Mrs. Day. "I know you won't tell on us."

Dolly Day smiled. Tell on Sue, the girl who had revived her interest in life? Or an old man who had given her the beauty of the November rose? "No indeed." Besides, she reasoned, she too would be a guest at the Cantrell home long enough to decide whether the old man should remain there or be moved along before she left.

They stopped at the Kirby home first to rid the car of most of Dolly Day's luggage. Only a faint light gleamed, but when Mr. Kirby came to the door, lights in his face, the living room and the porch burst into being.

He was reluctant to see Dolly drive away, but was left with the comfort of "a wedding in the Cantrell garden. Ned was always a friend of mine."

Sue stopped next at the library, drew her aunt to the doorway, quickly whispered a brief on their guests, warned her of Uncle Izzy's presence, then took her out so her greetings could sound natural to any waiting ears.

"I'll take them home, then come back for you," Sue assured her. "And remember Uncle Izzy is my father's mother's brother."

"Brother's father's mother," repeated Lovenia dutifully.

"Darling, he's not your grandmother; he's my f.m.b. Does that make it easier?"

"Oh, get on with you," ordered her aunt, laughing.

As tired as they were, they had a merry evening when Sue brought her aunt home. Lovenia agreed with Sue that the den would be ideal for Uncle Izzy and was excited at the idea of a wedding in her garden.

"Has Gypsy been in?" Sue asked.

Lovenia laughed, but unhappily. "Once. Milly was there. She came face to face with Gypsy and spat, 'No wonder you wear scarlet.'"

"Oh dear," breathed Sue.

"But wait. Gypsy smiled her lazy smile, leaned

forward and whispered, 'Psst, your breeding's showing.'"

"The one remark created to find the chink in Milly's armor," sighed Sue, "I hope Gypsy wears a suit of mail under her gay clothes."

They were having breakfast in the garden when Milly telephoned next morning. Sue, running in for hot biscuits, heard the shrilling of the bell and slowed to a walk. Wearily she answered.

"Sue? Milly speaking. Susan, I'm shocked and horrified at what you've done. I *don't* know what's gotten in to Lovenia to allow you such liberties."

Sue stared at the telephone, crushing an impulse to suggest Milly attend to her own sweet business.

"Well?" demanded Milly, "haven't you thought up an answer?"

"First I have to know the charge."

"Have to know?" shrilled Milly. "What but bringing those two unknown tramps into Lovenia's home? And don't try to lie out of it, Sue. I've caught you in a lot of untruths, you know. Clara recognized that mail-order bride in your car. I don't wonder the woman is trying to sneak in. Imagine a romance at her age; she's all of seventy."

"Seventy-four," Sue told her, "and admits it. Imagine a woman admitting her age, Milly. Refreshing, isn't it?"

"And that man. Why, Mel passed him tramping along the highway trying to thumb a ride."

"He's eighty-four," Sue informed her. "Imagine anyone not offering an old man a life. Uncle Izzy missed the bus and—"

"*Uncle Izzy!*" Milly's voice held such a note of horror Sue restrained her laughter with difficulty.

"Sue, you told me you had no relatives."

"No, it was Mel who put me through *that* third degree. I told him I had no *close* relations except Aunt Lovey. Uncle Izzy is a distant relation. On my father's side," she added.

"Well, I certainly want to meet him," Milly declared.

"And he wants to meet you." Sue could now speak the truth, something she felt was unusual in her contacts with Milly. "He says from what's he's heard of you, you must be unique."

"I'll be down. Later—"

After Aunt Lovenia and I have gone to the library, Sue thought as she slid the hot biscuits into a bowl, covered them and started out to the blazing beauty of the autumn garden.

Mr. Duncan never told anyone about his interview with Milly. Lovenia and Dolly drove into town with Sue, then went about preparations for the wedding, and Sue went happily to the library, glad to be back, enjoying afresh the cheerful big room.

She tacked up a sign announcing a fresh delivery of fiction and non-fiction was due the following day, filled the vases with flowers from the garden, talked to Agnes Kane and then went to her desk as the first borrowers appeared.

When she next looked up she saw Clara Carmandy talking with Mrs. Kane, and then saw her settle into a chair, facing Sue's desk, ready to take a knitting lesson. And Sue laughed.

She didn't laugh when she saw Gypsy Ladue come in. Gypsy was thinner and the shadows under her eyes deeper; even her clothes were subdued in color. Gypsy was dressed for the city, Sue sensed.

"Do you mind if I carry a book to read on the bus?" she asked.

"You know I don't."

"Escape," Gypsy admitted. "When my troubles seem more than I can bear, I read of other people's troubles as a counter-irritant. Sue," her voice lowered, "I'm going to visit my husband. He's at the state home. The scandalmongers of this town drove him there."

Sue was quiet with the silence of shock, then, aware of Mrs. Carmandy's eyes, asked softly if Ed were driving her down.

"Only to the Junction."

Sue scribbled a message on a card and tucked it in the book Gypsy had chosen. It read, "An old gentleman, Isidore Duncan, has a message of importance for you. He's at our home."

As she handed the book to Gypsy she said, "I hope you enjoy this."

There was a brief interlude of quiet; then Milly

Mack came in, danger signals flaming in her cheeks, dark eyes snapping, nails of the long hands tapping out a message of anger on Sue's desk.

"Never," cried Milly, "have I been so insulted. After all I have done for Lovenia, for her to allow a terrible old man to insult me as he did——"

"Was Aunt Lovenia home?" Sue asked warily.

"No. If she had been I'd have given her a piece of my mind."

Sue thought of Mr. Duncan. She couldn't imagine him being rude to anyone. "What did he say?" she inquired.

"Nothing," cried Milly, "not a thing. I asked him important questions and he refused to answer. And when I told him what I thought of him for sponging off a poor, pitiful old woman, he merely smiled and shrugged his shoulders."

"Didn't he comment on anything?"

"Once. When I said I had a right to demand an answer because Lovenia was deeply indebted to me and wouldn't be able to repay me if she had to feed indigents, he asked how much Lovenia owed me. I asked what business that was of his, and he had the temerity to tell me he had some savings and felt it only right he should repay me. Savings . . . that old . . . "

"Gentleman," murmured Sue softly.

"As though he'd have money enough. Well, if he's your uncle you're going to do what you please, but I trust for Lovey's sake you make his visit a short one."

She turned jerkily and went with her stiff legged walk out of the building.

A shadow fell on her desk and Sue looked up. Agnes Kane stood there, her hands trembling, her old face white. "Sue, Milly Mack is up to something. Clara Carmandy and I quarreled. She didn't come in for a lesson; she came in to watch you. And when she tried to make me talk about your affairs I—well, I guess I just told her what I thought of her, and now—"

"What could Milly do to you?"

"Nothing to me, but to my daughter Bella. I don't know, Sue, I don't know."

Sue found out that noon. Bella Kane came in, her face tight with worry. She looked first to make sure her mother had left for her lunch and that no one was near, then whispered, "Sue, I've been fired. Mr. King gave me a week's wages in lieu of notice and told me to leave. Sue, he accused me of immoral conduct."

"You?" Sue could have laughed in shocked surprise except that she knew the accusation of the gentle Bella sprang from something more sinister.

"I've been stepping out with Harold Peters; he's a teller at the bank. Sue, if I see him again I know Mr. Foss will discharge him. And oh, Sue, the payments on our home and —"

"Bella, listen. What's happened really has nothing to do with you. Someone is finding it necessary to show me her power by striking at someone close to me. Now don't worry. I can take care of your payments. I'll see your Mr. Peters and explain to him that it will be better not to call on you for a little while."

"But, Sue—"

"You need a good cry. Bella. Go down to Aunt Lovenia's and have a talk with Uncle Izzy. He has the grandest way of making you see things in their true perspective."

Sue was rushed for the next two hours. Her aunt was chaperoning Dolly Day, the two spending the afternoon at the Kirby place.

Sue bent over her work and worry assailed her. Money. She needed more money. Aunt Lovenia must have a new dress for the wedding.

"You look disturbed."

Sue saw books slide toward her, then looked up. It was the stylishly stout Mrs. Stump, Sally, who ran a small dress shop. Things were said about Mrs. Stump. She entertained traveling salesmen. Only last winter one had remained at her house for two weeks and she'd been known to buy a fifth of whiskey while he was there. Of course she'd bought lemons, too, and while that Doctor Foster had indignantly said the man was on the verge of pneumonia after a night in a stalled car— well, Mrs. Stump wasn't all she should be.

Sue was thinking of the final gossip. "And he young enough to be her son." Her smile at Mrs. Stump carried the regard she felt for a woman who'd sacrificed business to the care of a comparative stranger.

"I am," she replied, "I'm trying to figure ways and means of buying Aunt Lovey a new dress for the Day-Kirby wedding. You're coming, aren't you?"

"I wouldn't miss it for worlds. Aren't they the cute old couple? Got my girl workin' over some of them dresses Dolly bought in the city; hang on her like a coat on a scarecrow. Now I don't know your aunt's figure. She ain't never patronized me, but I don't hold that again her. Lord knows until you come she couldn't call her soul her own. But I'm markin' down summer stock and there's one little number would make her look the pure beauty. I'll bring it down tonight. Won't cost hardly nothin', and your credit's good."

Sue checked out Sally Stump's books, her eyes puzzled as she noticed the titles, not vivid romances but nostalgic first person stories of farm life.

Bella Kane came in to borrow Sue's car. Her cheeks were pink, her eyes sparkling, and there were one or two in the library whose brows arched until they nearly reached their hair-lines. Bella certainly didn't look like a girl disgraced and discharged.

"Your aunt's running her legs off," she reported. "I'm used to driving Hal's car, but of course I don't feel like borrowing it now."

She turned back to say she'd come after her

mother and then back after Sue. "And don't worry about the shopping; Uncle Izzy and I are taking care of that."

Later, as Mrs. Kane, all aflutter, went out with her daughter, Sue saw the Mack car pull in across the street, next to the green. Only one person was in the car and that was Melvin. And he just sat looking out on the little park.

Now what? thought Sue, her nerves growing taut.

She was ready to close. If those two women browsing over the pottery would only get out. She looked at them with more interest and found them to be two of Milly Mack's closest friends and was suddenly afraid.

One picked up a vase and carried it to the front door, then returned, saying, "Junk. Come on, Addie." And they started out to step back and let Melvin enter.

Nice timing, thought Sue.

"I'll just slip the latch." Melvin gave her his sidelong smile. "Only way I can be sure of having you alone."

"Rather a public place to be seeing me alone," Sue commented. "You could call at my home, you know."

"And have Uncle Izzy as a chaperone?"

"Uncle Izzy has been there only twenty-four hours," Sue reminded him.

Even as she spoke she remembered that silence

was the only weapon she could use against Mel and Milly.

Melvin straightened now, and Sue, who had once been interested in amateur theatricals, recalled that this gesture was often seen in the wings as an actor assumed the character he was to portray, the character he had been rehearsing.

"Sue, I'm tired of being kept in the position of being engaged yet not engaged to you. I want this settled tonight. We will be married Sunday."

Sue waited. Again this was no time to speak. She must know what lay beneath this shocking demand. She looked at Melvin and wondered if he could sense the shivering nausea such a thought brought to her.

She leaned back and turned on the overhead lights and knew they were revealed like figures in a show window, and then she took her stand before the switch so Melvin would have to throw her aside to reach it.

"Sue, you don't understand what I said, did you?"

Sue heard a car whiz by, then slow, and far away she heard it come to a stop. It could be Milly, or some of Milly's friends.

Now that the light revealed every line of Melvin's face Sue was shocked at the fright in his eyes and grim determination in his face. Why, he's desperate, she thought.

"Turn off the lights, Sue. Turn them off before I have to. Sue, you don't know what happens to me when I get mad. I'm mad then, Sue, not angry. If you knew . . . what was that?"

She'd heard nothing, nothing but the painful thumping of her heart. Should she consent to marry him if only to get rid of him now?

"I can't!" The words had come out against her volition.

He took a step toward her. "You mean I'm so repulsive—"

She must not let him think that. "Melvin, if we married we'd have to live with Milly. Milly and I would quarrel. I can't live a life like that."

"Ah," It was a long breath of relief, but he was coming closer. "Sue, tonight. We'll skip out in your car. We could go to Timberton; you're known there. Milly couldn't bring me back from there because you're known; they'd believe you. I could get a job there. I'd work. Oh, I can work Sue; I've worked like—"

He stopped short, then dove suddenly for the light switch.

There was an awful stillness in the room, a blackness and a waiting. Gradually Sue's vision adjusted to the sudden darkness; a high swinging arc light across the street sent fingers of blue light into the big room.

"I thought I heard something." Melvin spoke warily.

"Melvin, we're being foolish. Let's go out. Bella is coming for me in my car."

"No, she isn't." Melvin laughed. "A friend of mine called her and said she was bringing you home.

No, Sue, you have your choice of two answers: marry me Sunday or run away with me tonight."

She could pretend she'd run away tonight and, once she was outside, she could run away from not with Melvin.

"I'd need some clothes," she said thoughtfully.

"You've got money to buy clothes. We'll drive down to your place, leave Milly's car and pick up yours. Come on, Sue."

She didn't move. Suddenly this big room seemed a haven. If she went to the street, how far could she run before he would catch her? How loud could she scream? Would there be anyone on this lonely side of the square at the dinner hour? Anyone who would hear her? That car that had stopped. It wasn't Milly, or had Milly told Melvin to pretend to work against her if that would bring Sue to an agreement? How could you fathom such dark depths as the mind of Milly Mack?

And what did they hope to gain? If she could know that—

Melvin had moved to the door, adjusted the lock, after opening it, and now he turned swiftly and before Sue could realize his intent had scooped her into his arms.

He was strong. He had worked. Sue knew he had done years of manual labor for Milly Mack, saving her the waste of paying for outside help.

She'd wait until the door was pulled behind her, to then kick and scream.

"Put her down!"

Ed Weaver was suddenly between Melvin and the door, had pushed the door closed and turned on the lights.

Sue gave one tiny cry of relief and pain, for Melvin's arms were brutally tight.

"Sue and I are being married tonight," Melvin stated. "How did you get in? Sue, did you give this man a key? Are you and he——"

He stopped with a grunt. In one swift movement Ed Weaver had torn Sue loose from his arms and had Melvin by the arm, swinging him wide and turning to that swing to catch him as he turned back in a crouch.

"Why, you little rat. You little cornered rat!"

Sue saw Ed towering over Melvin, ready to drive him to the other side of the room with one blow. And in that instant she jumped for Ed's arm. "Don't!" she cried. "Ed, don't strike him."

Chapter Fourteen

In shocked amazement Ed turned to Sue, and in that instant Melvin struck him and Ed turned back to reach down and gather his shirt into a bunch and hold him off.

"Sue," he spoke over the head of Melvin, "you don't mean you love this——"

She tried to tell him with her eyes what she did mean, what she suddenly realized.

"Please see him to his car. I want to go home. I feel green."

"Nauseated?" he asked quickly. "Put your head down." But his glance said he understood.

"Come on, Roth. If you have anything further to say to Miss Thompson you say it at her home, later. I don't know what I got into here. Maybe some women like to be handled like a bundle of rags, but I certainly didn't think Miss Thompson would."

He freed Melvin, and after a moment Melvin turned to Sue. "You're right; this place is too public. I'll see you at Lovey's later." And then he turned to Ed Weaver. "You, I'll see in jail."

When he had left Sue whispered, "Walk to the telephone with me, the drugstore where we'll be seen. I'll call Bella to come after me. See over there in the park? Witnesses."

Weaver stifled a word, then breathed, "So that's why you wouldn't let me strike him."

"In jail on a battery charge, even intent to murder so no bail could be given, you'd have been of no use to your friends."

"A neat trap. I received a call you were in trouble. Oh, good evening, Mr. Foss."

"Weaver," snapped the banker. "Miss Thompson, are you walking my way?"

"She is," Ed answered for her, "but if you have

your car handy you'd be doing her a great favor to drive her home."

"My car? Why, yes, certainly, it's back on the other side of the square."

They turned about, and Sue saw the Mack car still parked across from the library. Weaver also saw it.

"I'll walk back with you," he said, "and follow in my car," he added thoughtfully.

Mr. Foss hesitated, then asked Sue earnestly, "Wasn't this the man who was bothering you?" And when she shook her head, "I was working late. Someone called saying something was wrong at the library; some man seemed to be bothering you."

"That's the message I received," Weaver said.

Mr. Foss lifted a hand and rubbed his brow with his thumb as though the pineal gland were an extra eye which might see into this situation. And then they reached his car and he ushered Sue in.

When they had driven off he looked down at the quiet Sue. "I was sorry to interfere, but you know of course Mr. Weaver served a jail sentence."

Sue felt as though he'd struck her. A jail sentence? Ed Weaver?

"Assault and battery," Mr. Foss continued. "I'd been favorably impressed by the young man; then this was brought to my attention. One doesn't admire young men with no control of emotions, or fists."

Sue sat up. "Mr. Foss, was that charge brought by Mr. Ladue? How long ago?"

"Why just after he came to Lakeville."

"And your same source of information didn't reveal that Mr. Ladue is now in a mental home? Mr. Foss, Ed Weaver could have been arrested for assault and battery tonight and, with a previous conviction, held there. Yet all he was doing was trying to protect me."

At the Cantrell home, only Mr. Duncan was in the living room when Sue entered. "The girls are upstairs talking gores and ruffles. Sue, you've had trouble?"

Surprisingly tears welled up and slid down Sue's cheeks. "Uncle Izzy, how can one person corrupt a whole town?"

"One person can't. Child, don't you realize evil is no more than a seed? It can't germinate unless it falls on receptive soil, and it can't grow unless it is cultivated. Lakeville has provided rich soil for evil and the people of Lakeville have spent their time cultivating it."

"Then how can one get rid of it?"

"You don't garden, but perhaps you can understand this. There is one species of oxalis, a reddish brown clover-like plant with tiny yellow blossoms. Once it is started in soil it crowds out the good grass and flowers. Its seed pods pop open and can then throw the seeds sixty feet.

"Scandal is like this oxalis, gossip the seed. It's easier to let it run rife than root it up. To clear a community would take concerted effort, because gossip, like oxalis, can spread further and faster and take root where nothing else will grow."

"Then I want to get out of Lakeville."

"Where would you go when even nations are throwing seeds of scandal?"

Sue dried her eyes and sat in dejection. "Then there isn't any answer."

"There is an answer to every problem. I'm trying to find the answer to Lakeville's. Tomorrow I shall visit the town and talk to the people."

Ed Weaver came while "the girls" were still upstairs, but aside from a reassuring pat on her arm and the answer to one question, Sue was excluded from his interview with Mr. Duncan, an interview that took place in the den.

To Sue's, "How on earth did you get into the library?" he replied, "Knowing how women could lose keys, Dupre had an extra set made and gave them to me. I thought they might come in handy sometime when I was in a burgling mood, so I kept them. All right?"

"Just so you don't lose them," Sue breathed. "I'll feel safer if I know they're on your key ring."

This is when she received the pat, "They will be, Susan, and the ring will be with me, always."

Milly Mack arrived while Ed was still in the den with Mr. Duncan, and Sue had moments of sheer agony lest he walk out before she left.

"I want to talk to you, alone," Milly stated, her black eyes feverish, her long hands jerking.

"Come outside; we'll take a drive."

"We can talk in my room," Sue countered swiftly, "or here. We won't be disturbed. Wait." She flew down the hall to the den door, to rap, open the door a crack and say, "Uncle Izzy, Mrs. Mack is here. She wants a private talk with me. Do you mind staying in there a little while?"

"Not at all," he assured her. "Take your time; I'm very comfortable." And she heard the gentle turn of the key in the lock.

She found Milly at the foot of the stairway, listening. And to her, "Who's up there?" Sue told her, then ran up the stairs to warn her aunt, Dolly and Mrs. Stump of Milly's presence.

When she came to the head of the stairs Milly was at the foot watching, a peculiar expression on her face. "Careful, Sue. You'll fall. You'll fall if you're not careful."

She found she could laugh and did. "Then you'd better move away, Milly. I'm heavier than I look. If I fall I'll land on you and splatter you all over the hall."

She fixed her mind on Ed Weaver taking the steps with his easy grace and kept it there until she was beside Milly.

"Sue Thompson, you hate me, don't you?" demanded Milly. "Don't deny it; I can see it."

"It is said," observed Sue, "that we see the world and others through the glasses we wear, glasses of our own making. I love the world too

161

much to look at it or the people in it through hate."

The implication set Milly back a little, but the moment they were seated she began a grueling half-hour. And Sue knew that Milly Mack was looking for information she could use against her brother.

"Sue, you're not telling me the truth. I know when you're lying."

Sue stood up. She'd had months of this, she had had enough.

"If you consider I only lie to you, there is no point in you questioning me further. If you'll excuse me I'll have my dinner. Aunt Lovey is upstairs."

Sue went into the gay red and yellow kitchen and stood shivering. She looked at the food her aunt had left to be warmed over and felt nauseated. If she could only get away for a little while, go some place where she could relax without fear.

And she knew there would never be any place, because wherever she could go Milly and Melvin could follow, and away from home there would be no one to help her against them.

Yet why did they concentrate on her? If she could find the answer to that.

Within the next few days, two brawls were started in the library. Sue was aware of one impending when she saw three of the town's hoodlums barge in and act truculent. She knew a moment's fear when she saw a young man move outside, then saw him pull down the corners of his lips and knew he was whistling of re-enforcements.

Within two minutes a burly mechanic from a nearby garage was blinking at a shelf of light romance, a bartender was blinking at a tome on Martin Luther he had pulled down, and a grocery clerk was staring at a book on garden flowers.

The fight began between the hoodlums. It began only. Instantly each man was taken by the seat of the pants and the collar, carried to the street and set down with orders to "work off your steam out here."

The second brawl was even shorter. Clara Carmandy tried to pick a row with one of the young Lakeville wives. Clara slapped the girl's face and the girl, with one swift movement, reached forward and pulled Clara's wide-brimmed hat down over her eyes.

By the time Clara could pry it up there was no one left in the library with whom to fight save Mrs. Kane, whose shoulders shook as she knitted, and Sue, who was bending down checking material in a lower drawer, marking time to control her laughter.

To Clara's wild cries of "Did you see that?" no one had seen anything.

Yet it was like sitting on a powder keg with the fuse lighted, Sue thought.

The wedding of Dolly Day to William Kirby was a quiet, lovely affair. The garden was at its autumnal best, the guests were few but warmly sympathetic. Isidore Duncan gave the grey-haired bride away, a very pretty bride, with Mrs. Stump bursting her seams with pride as her "little numbers" walked in review.

Sue was the only dark note. Sue, as bridesmaid, was wearing one of her formals, and she'd lost so much weight they had to gear it to her with safety pins.

That night the young Lakevillites placed an invisible guard around the home of the William Kirbys, and when the now well organized hoodlums arrived to shivaree, they left their cars on the highway for a quick get-a-way and were quickly rounded up by state police.

The next morning Sue sat at her desk running nervous hands through her hair. "What is it, Uncle Izzy? Why are these boys suddenly vicious? Within the last week they've set fire to the schoolhouse, broken the church windows and even invaded the post-office. Why?"

"They're bewildered, Sue," Mr. Duncan answered, "they've awakened to a world which offers them nothing but a chance to die in battle, and they're striking blindly at that world. They're made bold now by the unrest in their homes, the sense of insecurity."

"Well, thank goodness election is only four days away. Uncle Izzy, could you take over my desk while I run down and do our week-end shopping?"

"Gladly."

"You don't mind waiting for your daily browse among the Lakeville shops?"

"I've still enough time," he replied softly.

Sue puzzled over that thought as she started around the square. But she forgot it quickly. Her progress was slow. Everybody seemed on the sidewalks, gathered in knots or ones and twos, or waiting to waylay a listener.

Hands reached out to detain Sue, gripped her arm while words were thrown at her. She'd wrench herself free and move on, sickened, only to be caught by the next hands which held her until some story was told.

Why, she thought, these people have forgotten all about the real issues at stake. This is no more than a vicious campaign of personalities.

By the time she reached the library Sue felt shredded. She sank into a chair and looked at Mr. Duncan, misery in her eyes.

"Uncle Izzy, what would happen to Lakeville if everyone were forced to speak lovingly of everyone?"

Isidore Duncan sat up, alert. "Go on, Susan," he urged.

"I started around the square and I was stopped every ten feet by electioneers, which means everyone in Lakeville. At each stop pure poison was pumped into my mind. Doubt of this one's virtue, distrust of that one's honesty. Resentment at another's misrepresentation of me and mine. Hatred, all of it.

"If only there were some way to make each person turn what they were saying in a diametrically opposite direction, to speak with love instead of hate." She hesitated.

"But how, Sue, how could this be done? Gossip is a habit. Gossip is one of the worst of all habits. How could it be broken overnight?"

Sue looked across at the park green where a man lay propped against a tree. Lakeville's most hopeless alcoholic.

She tensed. "Alcoholics Anonymous. Scandals or Gossips Anonymous. The A.A.'s, I understand, work on a twenty-four hour plan. They are asked to abstain from alcohol only twenty-four hours at a time. If . . . Uncle Izzy, where are you going?"

Isidore had picked up his funny hard hat and was trotting toward the door. "Why, Susan, I am going to bring love to Lakeville."

Chapter Fifteen

Sue slept almost all day Sunday. It seemed strange the sleep she had each night wasn't enough, just as it seemed strange to know Ed Weaver spent the nights in the house though she never saw him.

It was a sticky hot day. Once when she awakened and went to the window to see black clouds piling up on the horizon, she felt a desire to crawl

166

under the bed as she had when she was a child during her first thunderstorm.

"Escape," she said. "Why, that's why I'm sleeping so much. My mind is tired and I'm trying to escape its eternal going around in useless circles."

She looked down. Bella Kane had borrowed her car for the day to take Uncle Izzy calling, she said. They'd been in for lunch and were now starting out again. Sue hoped they wouldn't be caught in the storm.

Slipping into slacks and a silk shirt, Sue went down to find her aunt at the telephone, her cheeks pink, her eyes laughing. "Yes, yes, do come over. Hurry so you'll reach here before the storm."

She hung up and, reaching for Sue, squeezed her shoulders. "Dear, that was Martha Dunne. Why, she hasn't spoken to me for years. And she's coming over, Sue; isn't that wonderful?"

Sue batted her eyes. Wonderful that a woman who hadn't spoken for years was coming over?

"Martha said she spent the first three years hating me because of a cruel story she'd heard I told about her. Then she spent the next three years hating herself for having believed the story. She's just reached the point of forgiving herself."

"Forgiving herself?" repeated Sue.

"Uncle Izzy says much of the grief of the world comes from not being able to forgive ourselves the wrongs we've done others."

Sue's taffy-colored hair swung as she shook her head. "That doesn't make sense."

167

"It does when you reason it out. Uncle Izzy says there's a law within us. Some people call it conscience, some subconscious and superconscious, some call it the spirit within and some call it God. When we've wronged another this makes us uncomfortable. It can't be hoodwinked by rationalization, nor bribed by condoning words of friends. It's like a law in chemistry. It can't be broken.

"It's easy enough to forgive others, but until we forgive, or make right with ourselves, that kernel of misery remains."

Now Sue nodded. "First we admit we were wrong, the most difficult of all things. And too few will, so they do good works as an emollient or bad works as a counter-irritant. Well, I'll snatch a bite of lunch and leave you to Martha."

As she walked away she murmured, "Uncle Izzy certainly gets around."

When she returned to her room she went to the east window and looked out on the approaching storm. It was a frightening thing, gigantic clouds boiling up beyond the hills and streaked with lightning, and the lake lying oily blue waiting the onslaught.

The lake and Ed Weaver were so closely associated thoughts of them ran together. And she felt part of the nervous strain she was under could be laid at his feet. Just as she had assembled all evidence of his loving Gypsy, he'd flash her a glance or do some thoughtful thing and she'd be mired down in her love for him.

Wind ruffled across the lake and Sue pulled down the window, and on second thought, childishly pulled down the blind.

From a north window she looked out over trees and up to the far hill where the Mack home was like a queer growth. She thought of Milly, and as though the thought had struck some note the first volley of near thunder started.

She was remembering a conversation she had overheard at the library. She knew now it had been meant for her ears, though then she hadn't caught the significance of it. "Milly's a changed woman since a certain person came to Lakeville." She had believed then they'd meant Ed Weaver.

Now, aware her slacks were slipping, she hitched them a bit. How thin she was getting. How much she had changed.

She and Milly Mack had changed since Lovenia Cantrell's niece had come to Lakeville.

Now that they were in juxtaposition she could see the symbolism. Just as Milly Mack was to her the symbol of an influence to be destroyed, so was she, Sue, a symbol to Milly Mack of something destroying her power.

If power through money was Milly Mack's god, would she submit to its destruction?

Sue chilled with an unnamed fear. So this was why she was being guarded? Others, such as Ed Weaver, had reached this decision earlier.

But what could Milly do? Murder was out of

the question; Milly was much too smart to put herself in such a position. Yet there was such a thing as suggestive destruction. The stairs and Milly's attempt to convince her aunt she was destined to have a stroke. There were always accidents.

Thunder and lighning arrived together, and the house shuddered as the air sizzled, the reading lamp Sue had turned on going out.

Sue jumped, then laughed, feeling a fool. Yet she must face this. If anything should happen to her, what would her aunt do?

She turned and raced downstairs with never a thought of steps, and when she reached her aunt and her guest remarked, "That made me think I'd better take out life insurance. How about you, Aunty; have you any?"

"No dear, Ned didn't believe in wives carrying life insurance, and I never thought of it afterwards."

Sue sighed her relief as she was introduced to Maude. Then it wasn't a copy of a life insurance policy, naming her as beneficiary, which Milly Mack still held.

Something nagged at Sue's mind, but in the spirited laughter of the two women she gave up all thought of anything but basking in the revived friendship.

At that she made her plans for the next day. She computed what her aunt would need to see her through if she, Susan, should die. And she laughed at herself for even considering it. Death was something that would happen to anybody else but her.

Uncle Izzy came home in the storms' lull, and they all retired early, anticipating a real rest in relief from the heat.

They awakened to a dazzling morning with a faint crispness in the air. "There will be days like this," Lovenia forecast; "then in a few weeks the sky will seem to thicken, the morning frosts give way to freeze, and one day we'll awaken to snow falling."

"I dread today," Sue confessed, as she left the house, "today and tomorrow. The day before and election day."

"Should we close tomorrow?" Lovenia asked, but Sue shook her head. "Not with everyone taking time off to vote."

"But the brawls," Lovenia said, "I hear Milly Mack has asked for county police protection."

Sue started early, her car filled with flowers Lovenia had rescued before the storm. But the storm would have streaked the windows and she'd have to find someone to clean them.

Driving up before the library, she saw two men before the place, armed with buckets and mops.

Warily Sue stepped from the car. She looked, then looked again. But it couldn't be. It didn't make sense. These men were laughing and talking as they worked. *These men hadn't spoken for years.*

"Morning, Miss Sue," called one. "We just got

through washing the windows of our shop and thought we'd keep in practice by doing yours."

"Got run out of our place," the other said. "Wives have taken over; they're rearranging the stock."

When Sue could catch her breath she used it to say, "How can I ever thank you?"

"Might give us a bouquet," suggested the first. "We've got a counter in the middle of the shop."

The middle of a shop where a walled partition stood? But this meant that must be torn down.

"We got out of the habit of growing flowers," the second said soberly. "We were staying behind our counters growing weeds."

"It's a day for flowers and shining windows," Sue agreed.

Sue tiptoed around the shop arranging flowers, tiptoed hurriedly but warily, as though some bubble she'd held for a moment might burst. There was still the vacuuming and dusting to do.

Agnes Kane was early. She came in, smiling. "I'll sweep, dear. Sue, guess what? I'm so happy I could sing. Bella's been called back to her old job and given a raise. In't that wonderful?"

The rank weed of suspicion sprang into Sue's mind. Bella had worked for a concern indebted to Milly Mack. Was Milly changing tactics?

And Mr. Foss, at this hour of the morning? He was going to the bank early, but he was coming here first.

Sue's heart contracted with fear. Then she saw his face and relaxed a little.

"Mrs. Cantrell not down yet?"

Again Sue's heart pinched.

"Good news this time, Miss Thompson; very good news. As you've been handling your aunt's affairs I am free to tell you. Former neighbor of your aunt's came over to my house at the height of the storm yesterday. Brought me a check for five hundred dollars. Ned Cantrell had loaned it to him years ago without asking security. Oh yes, he did loan it. I'm sure of that. I remember Ned withdrawing that amount from a savings account. I was a teller at the time and wondered what he would be wanting to do with that much."

Sue's heart did another convolution when, at her desk, she saw the full gang of hoodlums passing, punching one another, pushing those on the outer edge from the sidewalk, yanking shirt tails out, mussing hair.

When they stopped at the edge of the library she debated whether she should lock the doors or run for help. And then she saw Isidore Duncan ride up with the parish priest, the rabbi and a Protestant minister.

They pulled a roll of tape, stakes, axes and hammers from the car.

Sue's eyes all but bugged from her head when the bartender came panting up.

Agnes Kane nodded. "For the boys whose people have no faith," she remarked. "Yet, Sue, that's a wise choice. If Ted takes an interest there'll be no liquor slipped out to minors. And who knows what other effect it will have on Ted?"

"But what's going on?" Sue cried.

"Didn't you know? Your uncle didn't tell you? Someone left some money in trust for a boys' club to be erected where he thought it most needed, the boys to do most of the building themselves. You see by doing that they'll feel an ownership. The land was contributed. Enough for a tennis court and squash ball court behind; inside, a bowling alley, and next year a swimming pool. Of course they'll have to hurry to get the walls up before snowfall."

Sue's guard for the morning came in, a dazed look in his eyes. "I was forever getting here," he mumbled; "people kept stopping me. Darnedest thing, Sue, they wanted to shake hands. Said they'd just heard about my war record and were proud to have me in Lakeville. Y'know," he continued, puzzled, "the last time his highness the mayor spoke to me he said they didn't want tramps in Lakeville. Sue, what's going on?"

Sue shook her head. "I'm prepared for anything." And she recorded her shocks of the morning.

But she wasn't prepared for Clara Carmandy.

Sue and Lovenia had worked out a schedule which would give them both a certain amount of free time. Sue opened in the morning, her aunt appeared at eleven to free Sue for shopping and lunch, then they were both there during rush hours of eleven to two, Lovenia returning home to come back at four, the two going home together when they closed up.

Dolly Day's advent had disturbed their schedule, but it was now back in rhythm and Sue was planning to use her lunch hour to visit a life insurance broker.

Clara came before she could leave. Clara's eyes were red, her nose puffy, her lips pale, and Sue had to concentrate to hear the confession she blurted.

She wanted to apologize to Gypsy Ladue. Someone had told her Dick, Clara's husband, had left her because of that woman who lived at the county seat. She'd gone down to investigate, found the girl beautiful and also found her with Ed Weaver.

She hadn't found her husband or any trace of him, but she believed what she'd heard and someone had told her how to "get even" with Gypsy. It was she who had gone to Ladue with exaggerated stories. Now she realized what she had done and wanted to atone.

Sue's heart twisted painfully as Clara linked the names Ed and Gypsy, but she pushed her desire to know more away and instead asked a question. "Why and how did you lend yourself to such gossip and scandal?"

"I was never attractive," Clara confessed, "but I did have a quick and sharp tongue, and I found people liked to have me around as long as I could tell them something."

"Something cruel and harmful about someone they didn't like."

"That's it. Now I know that's why Dick left me. He said I was like a rattlesnake always shooting venom into someone. Miss Thompson, what can I do?"

"I don't know," Sue answered. "You might write Mrs. Ladue and ask if it would do any good to visit her husband and tell him you were wrong. But I'm afraid it's too late. I guess you'll have to go around doing as much good as you can in an attempt to offset the evil."

"But now that I realize, I can never forgive myself," sobbed Clara.

Sue left her in the little storeroom where they had had their talk and went out to find Isidore Duncan and send him to Clara. Then she went thoughtfully into the square.

There really wasn't any answer to Clara Carmandy, no relief unless it would be to tell her she was less evil than the person who had goaded her to her act.

"Careless talk." Sue didn't know she'd spoken aloud until two laughing voices took her up.

"Why—well—" said Sue, and looked at the man and woman in her path, hands linked. The two who'd been in the library that day, hating and loving each other with their eyes, separated by distrust born of gossip.

Prompted, she went on with her thought, this time aloud. "If a man or woman were to appear on the streets of Lakeville with a revolver in hand, shooting carelessly, they'd be put behind bars, the revolver confiscated. But these same persons can walk the streets shooting careless talk and sometimes the wounds are fatal."

They nodded solemn agreement.

"Tell me what's happened to Lakeville?" Sue asked.

"We only know what's happened to us," the man answered. "Each of us signed a pledge to speak and think only lovingly of everyone, to put every thought of animosity, resentment and revenge away for twenty-four hours. Well, two hours after I'd signed I was doing some heavy thinking and telephoned the wife."

"I'd signed an hour before he did," she laughed, and was sitting by the telephone trying to make up my mind to call him."

"I wonder what would happen to the world if everybody in it were forced to sign such a pledge, and then lived up to the requisitions."

"Be a wonderful place to live," the man said, "but unfortunately there would always be the few who were too steeped in their own evil to be able to live up to the requirements."

The Milly Macks, thought Sue, and felt again the chill of apprehension.

"I agree, however, these few would then stand

out in their own true colors and be easier to isolate and, if necessary, destroy."

"You have something there."

Sue hurried on. It now seemed more important than ever that she protect her aunt from ever again coming under the control of Milly Mack or her like.

And she wondered how Milly was feeling as she realized her pawns were all being moved beyond her reach, beyond her use. It would be like seeing her power withdrawn from her bit by bit. How would she react? Wouldn't she shut down on those held in her financial control?

Sue stopped at the edge of the square, a sudden vivid vision of Milly before her, a vision as real as though they were within arm's reach. Milly had been pacing the floor, pounding one fist into the palm of the other hand, and had come to a stop to look at Sue with murderous hatred.

When she started back toward the library, her signature on a contract, a check deposited with the life insurance agent, Sue found her chill of fear warmed by the love and laughter on the streets of Lakeville.

These people, more deeply indebted, some of them, to Milly Mack than Lovenia Cantrell, weren't afraid. Why should she be?

How many had heard of Scandals Anonymous? How many had signed the pledge? Or was it merely that the storm of the previous day had written the end to enervating heat and they were responding to the freshness of rain-washed air?

She had noticed several signs and stopped now to read one.

> Pre-election Rally in Courthouse Square
> Four o'clock this afternoon.
> Fifteen minutes only.
> Speaker—Isidore Duncan.

Now what was Uncle Izzy up to? Sue all but ran back to the library.

Sue reached there to find her aunt looking like the Cheshire cat.

"Sue, the most wonderul thing has happened. Uncle Izzy has paid off the mortgage in full. He gave me an unsecured—"

"You mean you gave him an unsecured note." Sue was laughing with her.

"At smaller payments than we were making Milly. Oh Sue, the relief. I could dance."

"Where is he now?"

"Out having lunch with the boys; look out the rear window."

She did. Isidore Duncan sat on an upturned box, in shirt sleeves, wind blowing his white hair, face alight with interest.

He'll founder, Sue thought, as Uncle Izzy accepted half-sandwiches, apples, pieces of pie and cake from the hoodlums.

She returned to her desk, surprised now at nothing but Uncle Izzy. Had he freed others from

Milly? But how? She had picked up a veritable tramp on the highway, an old man in a rusty black suit, and he was like a mite of leavening lifting Lakeville from its lethargy.

"Aunt Lovey—" she found a moment alone with her aunt— "have you seen Ed Weaver?"

"No, dear, but I understand some other young man has been coming in the last two nights."

Sue went back to her desk worried. With Ed Weaver within call, she wasn't afraid, but if he were gone on one of his unexplained trips, anything could happen.

They closed the library at a quarter of four to join the people massing the courthouse square. A happy crowd, Sue thought, and she thought of another rally that had been held early to avoid a riot. Yet here were people representing both sides of the political issue to be voted on the next day, and there was no sign nor sound of trouble.

There was a buzz of talk, then a roar of applause as the mayor appeared with Isidore Duncan. The mayor offered no eulogy, merely said, "Lakeville, here is your Uncle Izzy."

Sue lost the first words, so deeply was she withdrawn in her own thoughts, and then she saw a wave of something moving the people and opened her mind.

"We are inclined to forget we are a free people, so deeply do we become bound to our traditions and our prejudices. We will fight for our freedom

180

of action, but we accept chains that bind our freedom of thought.

"Tomorrow you will enact the ritual of freedom of thought. Let it be more than a ritual. When you enter the voting booth, pause to evaluate your relation to it. Think of the millions who do not have this sacred privilege. Above all . . . think.

"Too many have allowed their thinking to become atrophied like an unused member of their body. Too many rush to the polls, take a quick glance at the issue at stake, stamp their hurried reaction and rush back to personal life unaware their hurried action is part of a flood of reaction which will in time touch that personal life.

"As a stranger I do not presume to tell you how to vote, nor would I if I were an old resident. But consider your vote, analyze it, weight it, not for the effect it will have on tomorrow or next year but ten and twenty years hence.

"Your right to vote is a mighty anvil. Your vote is the powerful hammer that beats into shape the mold of your future."

Sue watched him turn away as deafening applause rang out; then she felt the now familiar clutch at her heart. Milly Mack was on the platform, Milly Mack with her arms outstretched, demanding silence.

Sue stood stiffly as Milly's voice rang out over the restless crowd, a noisy crowd now with shuffling feet and the sound of motors starting. She could hear only part of what Milly was saying.

"Admits he's a stranger." And "What right has he—" And again, "Do you want to put Lakeville in the control of a man who is here representing great interests that intend to ruin your land?"

The crowd was thinning, the noise growing. Still Sue stood rooted, unable to be one of those turning from Milly Mack, walking away from her, leaving her still talking, gesticulating.

"Sue," a high clear voice rang out, "you're needed at the library!"

Now that the others had moved away Sue was standing alone, her yellow dress vivid against the green. And Milly Mack had identified her and was addressing her in a voice of distilled bitterness.

"Sue," one of Lakeville's high school girls caught her arm and swung her around, "come on. You have customers lined up three thick."

And Sue walked away, one of the last to leave Milly and with her walked some sense of pity.

Everyone was surprised at the outcome of the election the next day. There was no cleavage between the old and the new. The school bond issue passed with a fine majority. Two former members were returned to the school board and one new one from The Oaks.

Even the losing member wasn't bitter but took his defeat philosophically. "Need some new blood," he said.

During the rest of the week Sue noticed two things. Her library guard was doubled and strange cars prowled the boulevard and side streets at night.

But there was no sign of either Ed Weaver or Melvin Roth, and Clara reported Milly had asked her to come up and stay while Melvin was off on a vacation, deer hunting. Clara had declined. She was enrolled in a nurses' aide class.

Mr. Duncan seemed forever busy, and Sue scarcely caught sight of him except at the dinner hour. Her own work was brisk, and she confessed, Saturday night, that she was looking forward to Sunday and intended to sleep until noon.

"Then have brunch with us," said Lovenia.

"Not us," Uncle Izzy said. "I'm dividing my digestion between three dinners, Sunday. If I survive I'll have a snack before bedtime."

She slept until nearly noon, awakened to see the noon time heat was as usual and donned a sun dress.

"I'll run out and set the table. Sue, you watch the coffee."

Sue smiled as her aunt went stepping along, new flowered house coat swirling above gay red slippers.

She turned off the heat under the coffee maker and picked up a tray. She'd take this out while the coffee filtered.

Halfway to the summerhouse she became vividly aware of the surpassing beauty of the day, the hot sun on the chrysanthemums, the brilliant blue of the Michaelmas daisies. And her aunt.

Lovenia Cantrell was standing in an unnatural position. She seemed frozen. Her eyes were closed, her face the white of death. And death lay coiled at her feet.

A giant diamond-backed rattler, ready to strike.

Chapter Sixteen

Later Sue would be able to separate the sounds which at the moment seemed woven into one.

There was the sound of a heavy body moving behind the summerhouse, the peculiar sound like that of a toy whirled on a stick which she knew intuitively was the rattle of the diamond-back. And then the horrifying blast of sound from behind her.

And she would know it was her instinctive move to protect her aunt which saved her. That the snake, hearing the crash of dishes and sensing the approach of an enemy from the rear, had held his strike to turn his head and investigate.

It was in that moment the shot came and Sue responded to the cracked order, "Stand still!"

Even as she watched the head of the snake disintegrate, the coils move convulsively, she heard a complaining, "I *had* to get his head," and someone rushed past her.

A bright blue shirt, a blond head and then the figure turned, Ed Weaver carrying the limp body of Lovenia Cantrell.

"Doc will be here in a minute," he said breathlessly. "She's all right; just shock. Thank God he taught her to freeze instead of run at the sight of a rattler."

He laid Lovenia tiptilted on the divan as Sue ran to the front door to let Doctor Foster in, then ran back with him.

"He didn't get in a strike?" were Foster's first words.

"No. That's why I had to get him in the head. I was afraid she'd collapse on top and give him a dying chance at her."

"Will she . . . is she . . . ?" Sue stammered.

"Psychogenic shock," Doctor Foster rumbled. "Miss Thompson, blankets and a hot pad for her feet." He was in the kitchen before she was, hypodermic in hand. "Adrenalin," he explained, and rushed back.

Other preparations were made, and when Lovenia's eyelids fluttered, Sue asked, "How'd you like to have a nice cup of coffee with a shot of brandy, Aunt Lovey?"

"Brandy?" asked her aunt between chattering teeth.

"You fainted, sweet. Next time don't wait breakfast while I sleep."

"Didn't. Sue, I'm going to be sick."

"Your privilege. Here's Ed to hold your heavy head."

They laughed and chatted in an easy way while she lay with waves of nausea beating at her. And then when she was ill, retching violently, they quieted, and she could look up at last and say to Weaver, "You act like you'd had a lot of experience."

"I was in the army," he teased.

She remembered then, but the hot coffee and brandy were spooned into her mouth, her limbs rubbed, and the warmth inner and outer quieted the chill.

They left her with Doctor Foster and went into the kitchen to make fresh coffee.

"Where's Melvin?" Ed asked.

"Supposed to be deer hunting. Why?"

"Snake hunting. Look." And he handed her a telegram. "This just arrived."

Sue read first, Deep Valley Snake Farm, then the message. "Man answering the description here Wednesday. Purchased six diamond-backs for museum, he said. I was away. Just learned of purchase."

"Six." Sue looked down at the floor as though she expected another coiled rattler.

"Five left," Ed answered soberly. "Sue, we've got to get you and your aunt out of here until it's safe. The only spot I feel is safe is the log house. But how to get you there without Milly knowing? That blasted telescope."

186

Sue remembered then the sound of the heavy body moving in the leaves behind the summerhouse. "It would be Melvin," she imagined. "Then if I were to telephone Milly and ask for Melvin I might be able to hold her to the telephone long enough to get Aunt Lovey into Doctor Foster's car. He could pull into the back drive; that's pretty well covered."

"Good. I'll have my boys scour the grounds and the outbuildings as unobtrusively as possible. Then you?"

Sue stiffened. "I'll drive out. I'll pick up Uncle Izzy, say he's wanted at Junction City and head that way, then turn off. Milly can't see The Oaks road."

And then Sue's head snapped up. "But why should we have to run from Milly after this?"

"Could you prove that snake out there was put there by Melvin? That it was a snake he purchased? They've probably got one to cover in case it was questioned. You'd find Melvin with six rattlers. Only you wouldn't find Melvin. Remember, he's deer hunting."

"Then we're going to sit idly by?"

"Sue, there has been no sitting nor idleness for months. At first we were handicapped by not having the necessary funds to make the proper investigation of Milly's and Mel's back trail. We have now. Give us a little more time."

Sue turned the flame low under the old coffee pot that had replaced the broken glass one she'd dropped in the garden. "That wire from the snake farm?"

"Part of the protection. Milly overplayed her hand when she planted that book where your aunt could see it. Milly wanted her to pass out in a public place so it could be proven later that she was deathly afraid of rattlers. That tipped us off to a possible plan. That's why Foster drilled her in snake lore. You know she could have died of shock with her previous fear of snakes.

"I canvassed every snake farm with a description of both Milly and Melvin, believing they wouldn't dare give that job to anyone else. But let's get out of here as soon as possible. We haven't accounted for the other five."

Sue brought coffee to the doctor, served herself and Ed, then, as they went back to the kitchen, asked one more question.

"Why Aunt Lovey?"

"That paper Cousin Hettie referred to in her postscript. I—wait, there's one of the boys. Sue, I may not see you for some time. But you'll be safe. As soon as you're in The Oaks, in our house, you'll be safe."

He was gone. Our house. So Gypsy was giving up the cottage he'd bought her.

Sue rushed to pack bags, her aunt's, her own and one for Mr. Duncan, and then with one of Ed's friends going before them, they escorted the still weak Mrs. Cantrell to Doctor Foster's car.

Sue put her own bag and Mr. Duncan's in her

car and went out shortly afterwards, feeling small prickles running up and down her spine and ridiculing herself, for now Lakeville was no longer a town of a thousand eyes working for Millie Mack.

Isidore Duncan was quick to respond to Sue's message. "That will be Don," he said, and turned to his hostess. "I promised to take Sue and her aunt to Don's mountain resort as soon as he had vacancies. They need a vacation. You found someone to take over the library, Sue?"

Sue looked shocked. She had forgotten all about library, gift shop and Mrs. Kane's knitting classes.

"You didn't see Genevieve Sharp? Well, we'll call her in town."

In the car he told her placidly he'd been sounding out the young folks to learn if there was anyone who could take over in case of emergency.

"And now tell me about the emergency," he suggested.

Sue related what had happened. "But I don't understand how they could be so stupid. There are no rattlers around here."

"Used to be. In fact, they were talking about it the other day. Folks thought they were returning to the valley. Several seen the last few hot weeks. Seems they come down to the water in long, dry seasons."

Sue told him then of her brief telephone call to Milly, Milly's voice, kinder than it had been of late, warm and full of concern. Someone had told her they'd seen that doctor's car.

"Uncle Izzy, if I had to keep on with Milly I'd forget how to tell the truth. I told her I'd gone out to the summerhouse and found Aunt Lovey in a faint, that she couldn't remember what had happened when the doctor revived her but that I was having car trouble and thought Melvin might drive me to Junction City, that I was taking her away on a vacation."

"Did you tell her where?"

"I told her it was out of Timberton, I'd write her the address."

The old man rumbled with laughter. "Too bad you didn't reach this town sooner."

They drove on, after turning the keys over to the girl whom Sue now remembered, but she didn't feel safe until they were entering The Oaks, nor until those who'd followed leisurely pulled in after her and said there had been no sign of anyone watching.

When they came to the log house they found it bathed in the last of a chill sunset. To Sue it looked strong and impregnable. It had also lost its look of a barracks. And inside, the curtains, drapes and cushions of her choosing gave it a feeling of home.

Gypsy met them at the door. "Your aunt is practically well," she reported. "She insisted on me finding a book of snake illustrations. She called it 'laying her ghost.'"

And then, as they'd entered from the rear, she said, "I hope you'll like what I've done. Now I must run. I want to bring some groceries over. I heard you'd thrown your lone meal of the day into a flower garden. Reminded me of the time Mother tried to force Ed to eat oatmeal. He carried his bowl to the garden, dumped the mush and jumped on the bowl."

She was off in a streak of scarlet skirt and jumper, Sue staring after her, repeating, "The time Mother tried to force Ed—" Her spirits rose. But when she went in to find her aunt relaxed before a log fire and Lovenia said, "I suppose *they* are waiting for Gypsy's divorce," her spirits dropped again. Ed could have boarded with Gypsy's mother who tried to make him eat oatmeal.

The days of waiting were sheer agony to Sue. She was falling more and more in love with the house. She couldn't help moving things here and there, seeking the acme of comfort.

Bulletins came from Lakeville. The first week was comparatively quiet. Milly Mack had appeared at the library and tried to learn Sue's whereabouts. Without success.

The second week Lovenia was asked to rent the house to two of the new schoolteachers. She would be allowed to live there as guest. Which was one way to defy the zoning law.

The second week, too, Milly Mack, it was learned, appealed to the state police. Her brother

191

Melvin Roth, who had gone deer hunting, had disappeared. She feared foul play.

Sue listened to this as she checked a report on the shop and the library. All three departments were picking up momentum; knitters beginning Christmas gifts, parties bringing buyers to the gift shop. And with colder weather creeping swiftly in, there was more time for reading.

The third week there was a definite change in the weather. The frosts of the morning remained all day. Then came the freezing of the ground as the sunlight became more and more remote until one day the sun was obscured by a gray film.

Milly Mack disappeared that week. The hired man, who said she hadn't reported she was going to visit, had run out of food for the stock and Mrs. Mack kept the keys to the storeroom. He had walked to a neighboring ranch and had the owner telephone Lakeville.

It snowed that day.

And Ed came home. Ed and Gypsy, who had not returned to the log house after that first evening.

Sue tried to read his face as he came in. He seemed utterly weary, yet there was a sense of accomplishment.

"You're hungry," Sue said.

"And tired. But later, after I have everything off my chest."

They gathered around the fire watching snowflakes filter down beyond the ruddy-draped windows, Sue, her aunt, Gypsy, Mr. Duncan and Ed

Weaver. And with each word Ed spoke Sue relaxed and wondered how she could have been so blind.

"I'll have to begin at my beginning," he said. "I was born in Chicago. When I was three my father died. Later mother married Demarset whose home was in New Orleans. Naturally I went down with them and remained there until I was ten. Gypsy was five then. Her name was the same as mother's, Lorraine, but because of her flair for bright colors we started calling her Gypsy.

"Mother died when I was ten, and as Demarset had been having a rugged time, Mother's brother offered to give me a home and educate me. So I went back to Chicago. Demarset moved several times, and you know how kids are about writing. I soon lost track of my stepfather and half-sister.

"During my summer vacations I took a job on a Chicago newspaper, and like most cubs had to take the mortuary beat. One of my first stories of any importance was covering the inquest of an old woman who had died of a heart attack under rather peculiar circumstances. She left property and life insurance to her companion-maid, a young woman named Minnie MacDonald.

"Like most reporters, I have a photographic memory.

"The maid was brought in for questioning, and because there was something peculiar about her to me, I photographed her in my mind.

"As there were no friends or relatives to make a

193

fuss and the coroner's inquiry established the cause of death, there was no reason for mugging or fingerprinting her.

"I finished Northwestern and went into the service. By that time my uncle had died and I was feeling pretty lonely. I had no next of kin. I'd thought a lot of Gypsy when I was a kid, so I appealed to the Red Cross to help me trace her.

"They had no luck until after I came back from overseas, then gave me the possibility of a Mrs. Antonio Ladue, living out here. I was working on a trilogy at the time and let things ride until I was through with it this spring; then I started out looking for her.

"I found her at county seat trying to rehabilitate a badly battle shocked husband, discharged from the army hospital. Because he was insanely jealous, part of his feeling of insecurity, we didn't try to introduce me. Gypsy—remember she was five when I'd left—had almost forgotten my existence and had not previously told Tony about me. To introduce a brother at that late date would take doing.

"I wanted a place close enough to keep an eye on her, yet not too close, so someone suggested Lakeville and I moved out here, and became interested in the town's problems, settling at The Oaks.

"One day I came into town, to the city hall, to help one of the boys secure a business license. I'd heard some woman who practically owned the town and was fighting it.

"I think I knew instantly that Milly Mack and Minnie MacDonald were the same. When I saw her pounding a fist in a palm I had no doubt. The companion-maid had done that.

"I doubt she recognized me. I had been one of a group of newsmen, wearing hats, and ten years had passed, but I'm sure she saw something in my eyes that made her guilty soul know I had identified her from some place. For from that moment on she bent every effort to discredit me. Not openly, but in her own sweet, subtle way.

"That's how she caught me meeting Gypsy on the sly, and sent her henchwoman to Tony, destroying everything hospital and Gypsy had done. I think she hoped Tony would kill me. He tried, but we managed to hush that up and smuggle him into a state home, because we wanted him kept away from anything military.

"But before this and because of my first meeting with Minnie-Milly, I became interested in lonely people with whom she associated. I had a feeling Mrs. Cantrell was marked for a victim, but I had nothing upon which to move to protect her.

"Then Sue came to Lakeville and I complicated everything by falling in love with her."

"A nice time to tell her," put in Gypsy as Sue drew a sharp breath.

"She knew it," Ed said easily. "Minnie-Milly did."

Lovenia leaned forward. "Is that why she faked the engagement of Sue to Melvin?"

"One of the reasons; the other: she was beginning to fear Sue's intelligence and she wanted to force an open door into the Cantrell residence. Engaged, and she was sure Sue wouldn't dare deny it because of you, Mrs. Cantrell, Melvin would always have the right of entry to your house no matter how bitterly she and Sue quarreled.

"With Milly getting out of hand and you and Sue in danger, I had to do something, find some means of tracing Milly, get some charge against her that would check her. It was a costly job and with other commitments—"

"Meaning me," offered Gypsy.

"—I couldn't afford it, and I was afraid to leave you two in Lakeville without my eagle eye. I'd banded the guys at The Oaks into an emergency body. I could tell them some of my fears but—" He looked at Sue so imploringly she had to look quickly at the fire.

"Then I remembered a fine philanthropist I'd met during newspaper days. He'd once remarked if I ever found a town upon which he could work an experiment, I should let him know.

"I sat down and wrote him the whole story, he came up and we parked him in Junction City, after his arrival, until he could chance to meet Sue and, we hoped, be brought to the Cantrell home so he could guard from the inside."

Sue flashed a look of indignation at her Uncle Izzy and he chuckled. "Just an old wolf, Sue."

"Mr. Duncan also hired a force of private detectives to check Milly-Minnie's past.

"Now here's a peculiar thing. Milly has grown rich on inherited money, wisely invested of course, yet in not one single instance could there be any proof of murder. She would move into a town, become acquainted with some lonely, usually old woman, help her financially and then not ask but psychologize the woman into making out a will with herself as sole beneficiary."

They all stopped at Lovenia Cantrell's gasp.

And Sue cried, *"That's* the paper Cousin Hettie —Ed, why didn't you warn us?"

"It was too late to change Milly Mack. I know now I should have forced you into retirement somewhere away from her, but I thought we had you completely guarded. I did have. My guard for that day ran into car trouble. We can prove someone deliberately fouled his car, but not who. Instead of calling someone to take his place, he tried to get it fixed.

"That proves Milly Mack knew you were guarded and had checked the rotation. She was getting pretty desperate. I believe she checked with the Chicago newspaper and learned an Ed Weaver had worked there at the time she committed her first murder."

Lovenia spoke then. "But my will only gave her

as much as I would be owing at the time of my death."

"That's what you thought you signed. I've seen the will."

"Where?"

"At Milly Mack's house, this morning. Actually the document you signed gave her everything. By arranging accidental death for you, Milly could have stripped Sue of everything she had, run her out of Lakeville. That's what she wanted more than anything. Sue to her had become the symbol of loss of power; she wanted her alive so she could triumph over her disgrace, publicly."

"But, Ed, you mentioned that paper that Sunday."

"I was surmising but pretty sure. I'd talked to a lawyer who'd drawn up two. The first one Lovenia ordered; the second had corrections written in what he'd thought was Lovenia's hand. He was too much under Milly's sway to deny her when she said not to bother reading it aloud to Lovenia, they were in a hurry."

Lovenia Cantrell nodded. "I'd mislaid my glasses, I thought; actually they were broken and had to have new ones made. Milly paid for them."

They were quiet a moment; then Sue asked, half afraid of the answer, "Did you find Melvin?"

"The state police found him, not for Milly but for us. Melvin made a full confession of his part in the attempt upon Mrs. Cantrell, and confessed murdering Milly's husband. That was the hold she had on him."

"But he couldn't have been old enough."

"He was sixteen. He's twenty-six now, you know."

They didn't know and paused to consider what he'd said.

"Melvin's name is no more Roth than Milly's is Mack. His name is Mohr. Actually he's Milly's adopted son, though not legally. Milly married Bard Mohr, a well to do rancher who advertised for a housekeeper. Milly applied, got the job and eventually a husband. Melvin was Mohr's son.

"I imagine Milly worked up bad feeling between father and son in her subtle way, pampering Melvin to win him and setting him against his father. There was finally a scene between the three of them in a den Milly had fitted up for Melvin, in a tank house. It wasn't steps, but a ladder he had to go down.

"Melvin doesn't remember pushing his father, but he says he was so mad he could have, and Milly swore he did. We think she was responsible. There were two other cases where old women died of broken necks, accidental of course. Milly was no place around."

"If she wasn't, then she knows she was guilty of their deaths," Sue cried. "That's why she wouldn't have stairways in her house."

"Guilty, or afraid someone would do to her what she'd done to them."

He went on again. "Milly had been quite plump up to then, but the inquest of Mohr's death turned her hair white and turned her into the matchstick she is. Of course this didn't happen overnight. She still looked as she had when she and Melvin, completely cleared, collected the benefits, sold the ranch and disappeared.

"Milly now had almost everything she had been working towards. With Melvin she secured the far country for a town on which to work her will. Stopping at a dilapidated motel one night, she ran into Cousin Hettie, working there as a maid.

"She made an investigation of Cousin Hettie, learned she'd served a term for petty theft. She then arranged a second theft in an adjoining cabin, and when the irate occupant found the goods in Hettie's room, Milly stepped in and saved Cousin Hettie.

"Cousin Hettie confided she'd been framed twice but that *they* had believed her guilty because she had been trying to raise tax money on an old farm she'd inherited. She'd never seen it but had been trying to sell it.

"The old farm is the present Mack home which Milly purchased from Cousin Hettie for one dollar and the assurance of a home the rest of her life.

"So Milly Mack-Mohr and Melvin, now renamed and called a brother to allow Milly to be younger than she was, came to Lakeville. Milly with two slaves; one a so-called murderer, one an accused thief with a sentence served.

"And Lakeville was waiting for a Milly. Full of spite and envy, it provided a hotbed for the seeds she was preparing to sow."

He stopped as though he were through; yet still they waited until Sue spoke.

"But now that you've gathered all of this evidence which proves these deaths were more than accidental, the authorities will take steps to prosecute Milly, won't they?"

Weaver shook his head.

Indignantly Sue cried, "But she can't go on living—a menace."

"She won't, Sue. She isn't living. Milly murdered herself."

"Suicide? Milly?" came the chorus.

"No, murder, the murder she'd planned for your aunt. We found the other rattlesnakes this morning. Because of a short, the heat in the sunroom had been off for several days. The snakes were torpid and easily handled. We put them back in the carrier Melvin had left in the sunroom, and from which they had escaped.

"We won't know how nor if it was intentional. If Melvin released the latch, or if it was the hired man with his bitter grudge, or if it was accidental.

"Reconstructing, we know only that Milly came into the sunroom, evidently from the terrace. The room was hot and the snakes active. She might have stepped on one. She tried to run, caught her foot in a lamp cord—that caused the short—was thrown and must have been knocked

201

out. She was badly bitten by the snakes. And she was conscious before she died. Conscious, and b then helpless, with time to review her life."

Gypsy gave forth a great shuddering sigh, then jumped up. "Sue, do you mind if I make some coffee? I must have something after that horror."

"I mind?" Sue asked, bewildered.

"Well, darling, it's your house." She faltered and looked at her brother. "Ed Weaver, there are times when I wonder why I admit any blood relationship to you."

"It's puzzling. Sit down, Sue, and I can brew coffee that won't stand by its own strength."

Sue wondered if her knees would carry her into the kitchen. She paused just inside, puzzled by the radiance of the place, then realized it was reflection from the snow outside that turned the curtains golden, lighted each shining surface.

"Do you like it all right?" Ed asked anxiously "You knew I built it for you, didn't you?"

And now it was Sue who was exasperated. " am *not* psychic."

"But, Sue, you almost foretold every move c Milly's. When I came in to warn you, you'd literally lifted the words from my lips. Then why—Sue you didn't think Gypsy and I—"

"I didn't think what Lakeville thought. I ju didn't see how anyone could help being head ove heels in love with her. And you certainly gave m no encouragement."

She stalked to a shelf and took down a canni

ter, a white cannister with golden poppies, snatched at the coffee maker and began measuring in coffee.

Ed followed after a moment and grasped her wrist. "Wait, Sue. You're not from Louisiana; you don't like coffee stew any better than I. As for encouraging you, what do you think I've been doing these last two months? As soon as I got Gypsy settled I spent every minute of every day trying to get you and your aunt out of Milly's coils."

Sue frowned. Actions, not words? "But you didn't *say* anything. And why couldn't you have told me about you and Gypsy?"

Ed dropped her wrist, and Sue began shoveling coffee back into the cannister.

"We couldn't tell anyone, Sue, without endangering them. Tony is quite mad. He managed to break out once. Fortunately he was caught in time. There is no reason in a madman's mind. As long as he believed he had only to kill Gypsy and me, everyone else was safe. Had anyone attempted to tell him we were brother and sister, something Gypsy had failed to reveal in their brief marriage before he went into action, he would have turned on them as quickly.

"It was better to wait."

Sue set the coffee pot on a burner. "And now?"

"Poor Tony is in solitary. He's also a sick man. Gypsy won't have too long to suffer with him, vicariously. Now it's only a matter of weeks. And with the heavy snows, another escape in his condition isn't possible."

They waited a moment. "You might turn on the burner, then turn around so I can see your face."

Sue snapped at the burner, her cheeks crimson. "You forget I'm engaged." Then she did turn "Melvin—what will they do to him?"

"There's no proof he knocked his father from the tank house. Everyone believes it was Milly, just as they blame Milly for the snake. I think they will keep him under observation for a year or so, then, if we agree, free him to go some place far away from Lakeville. And you've never been engaged to him.

"Sue, I've been waiting ever since I pulled you out of the lake looking like a drowned rat."

Sue doubled her head over onto the broad chest just as she'd dreamed she was doing a thousand times. Only now she was laughing. Ed Weaver was definitely not a man of honeyed phrases.

But he was a man of action. It was Sue who had to break away as the coffee went boiling over the top and down on the gleaming porcelain surface of the stove.

The swing door opened and Mr. Duncan peered in. "Did I smell coffee? Ah, I see I did. Sue, you look radiant."

"Reflection of the snow."

"Ha. Ed, Gypsy says she'll be glad to have me as a star boarder. Agreeable to you?"

"A relief and a joy."

Sue turned to Mr. Duncan. "Uncle Izzy, remember the day you hurried out and said you were going to bring love to Lakeville? Well, you did, but how?"

"Well, in so far as I could I relieved their financial burden, in some instances, financial slavery, gave them a fighting chance to catch up. They will. From each I exacted a pledge, the pledge of Scandals Anonymous. In other instances I simply discussed hypothetical situations with individuals.

"Most people would rather live in harmony. Gossip, backbiting and scandal are habits, little ones that grow into big ones.

"I find that a lot of Lakeville people are renewing their pledge daily, breaking the bad habit."

"Will they keep it, all of them?"

"No, that would be too much to expect. But scandal will no longer be the principal industry of the town. Speaking of love coming to Lakeville, will I have time to send out for decent wedding garments?"

"No," declared Ed, "I've wasted too many weeks of worry. I'm not letting her out of my sight. By the way, why the disguise?"

"People are less suspicious of the inconspicuous." He moved forward and picked up the tray Sue had ready. "I'll leave you to make more coffee."

And Ed Weaver made the only romantic speech of his life as he gathered Sue into his arms. "Who wants coffee when he can have ambrosia?"

LOOK FOR OUR MAGNUM CLASSICS

ADVENTURES OF PINOCCHIO by Carlo Collodi
AESOP'S FABLES by Aesop
ALICE'S ADVENTURES IN WONDERLAND &
    THROUGH THE LOOKING GLASS by Lewis Carroll
AROUND THE WORLD IN 80 DAYS by Jules Verne
AUTOBIOGRAPHY OF BENJAMIN FRANKLIN
    by Benjamin Franklin
BLACK BEAUTY by Anna Sewell
CALL OF THE WILD by Jack London
"CAPTAIN COURAGEOUS" by Rudyard Kipling
CHRISTMAS CAROL by Charles Dickens
EREWHON by Samuel Butler
FIRST MEN IN THE MOON by H. G. Wells
FRANKENSTEIN by Mary Shelley
GREEN MANSIONS by W. H. Hudson
HAMLET by William Shakespeare
HANS BRINKER: OR, THE SILVER SKATES
    by Mary Mapes Dodge
HEIDI by Johana Spyri
HOUND OF THE BASKERVILLES by A. Conan Doyle
INVISIBLE MAN by H. G. Wells
ISLAND OF DR. MOREAU by H. G. Wells
JFK: A COMPLETE BIOGRAPHY 1917-1963
    by William H. A. Carr
JUST SO STORIES by Rudyard Kipling
KIDNAPPED by Robert L. Stevenson
KING SOLOMON'S MINES by H. Rider Haggard
LEGEND OF SLEEPY HOLLOW & OTHER STORIES
    by Washington Irving
LOOKING BACKWARD by Edward Bellamy
LUCK OF ROARING CAMP & OTHER STORIES
    by Bret Harte